Contents

An overview of our books for older, catch-up readers

Titan's Gauntlets is an engaging phonic reading series that, together with The Magic Belt, Totem and Talisman 1 & 2 series, provides dramatic quest stories for older, catch-up students. Right from the very beginning, the reader is swept along on exciting adventures while learning to read, following step-by-step phonic progression. The table below shows the over-arching structure of the five series and how they interlink.

Series	Suitable for	Who is it aimed at?	What does it cover?
Introductory Workbook	Readers aged 8–14	Absolute beginners. Students with shaky knowledge of the sounds and letters of the alphabet, who would benefit from starting a phonics program from the very beginning	Sounds and letters of the alphabet within CVC words
The Magic Belt reading series (12 books) and workbook	Readers aged 8–14	Students with prior knowledge of the sound and letters of the alphabet	VCC, CVCC, CCVC, CCVCC words and consonant digraphs ch, sh, th, ck, ng, wh, qu, and suffixes –ed and –ing
The Totem reading series (12 books) and workbook	Readers aged 8–14	Students able to read a simple text at CVC level and who know most of the consonant digraphs but have poor knowledge of vowel digraphs	A re-cap of words from CVCC level all the way to CCVCC level and of the consonant digraphs. Introduction of alternative spellings for vowel sounds, e.g. the spellings <ai, ay, ai and a> for the sound 'ae'
Talisman 1 Series (10 books) and workbook	Readers aged 8–14	Students who have poor knowledge of the phonic code and alternative spellings for vowel sounds	Re-cap of alternative spellings covered in the Totem Series and additional alternative spellings for new vowel sounds
Titan's Gauntlets (10 books) and workbook	Readers aged 8–14	Students who have poor knowledge of alternative spellings for vowels, consonants and common Latin suffixes	Alternative spellings for further vowel and consonant sounds and common Latin suffixes
Talisman 2 Series (10 books) and workbook	Readers aged 8–14	Students who have poor knowledge of alternative spellings for vowels, consonants and common Latin suffixes	More complex alternative spellings for vowel and consonant sounds and common Latin suffixes

Notes on Titan's Gauntlets Series and Workbook

Titan's Gauntlets Series

Introduction
Titan's Gauntlets Series continues from the Talisman 1 Series with the introduction of further spellings for vowel and consonant sounds and common Latin suffixes. (Titan's Gauntlets Series precedes Talisman 2 series, which revisits and expands on Titan's Gauntlets.) To see the phonic progression of the series, see the table on page 4. This workbook complements the series and includes a variety of activities to encourage the reader to practice reading and spelling, using the phonic knowledge and skills introduced in the books. It also offers engaging comprehension activities within the context of an exciting quest.

Suffixes
Book 7 introduces suffixes with complex spellings. At this point, they are taught as one syllable as they can be added to root words to make many long words in English. This enables the reader to read and spell many new difficult multisyllabic words. To see the introduction of suffixes and their spellings, see the table on page 4.

More text in Titan's Gauntlets Series
Titan's Gauntlets Series introduces more text to a page than in Talisman 1 Series. The purpose is to gradually extend the amount of text per page that the student can read as he/she progresses.

Order of the books
Titan's Gauntlets Series should be read in the numbered order. The phonic focus in each book becomes gradually more difficult, ending with complex suffixes.

Pronunciation
At the beginning of each book, there is a word list to help the reader learn the alternative spellings of the sounds and suffixes. Pronunciation of some sounds may vary, according to regional accents. The word lists may not always match the pronunciation of the student. This point should be discussed and the lists adapted to the student.

Blending, not guessing
Encourage the reader to use his/her phonic knowledge to blend the sounds fast throughout the word. If there are spellings he/she does not know, point to the part of the word that is new and tell the student the sound. Then, ask the student to blend the sound into the word. As he/she works through the Phonic Code, the student will be able to use this phonic approach successfully with an increasing number of words.

Teaching alternative spellings
The English Phonic Code is complex. This series presents a number of alternative spellings for sounds and for suffixes. The teacher may need to introduce these spellings gradually if the student has difficulty learning all the alternative spellings at a time.

Splitting multisyllabic words
It is important to teach students how to split multisyllabic words to enable them to use successful and independent strategies when reading and spelling long words. This workbook allows the teacher to use any method he/she is teaching the student.

New vocabulary

Each new book offers an opportunity to learn new vocabulary on the Vocabulary page. This page explains the words as they appear in the context of the story. The teacher may wish to discuss additional meanings of the words with the student.

The workbook

This workbook complements the Titan's Gauntlets Series. Ten chapters in the workbook correlate to the ten books in the series. Each chapter offers activities based on the phonic focus of each of the books. Before reading the books, students would benefit from practicing the knowledge and skills needed to read the book independently. This includes the word building, blending, reading and sorting activities which feature at the beginning of every chapter. Follow-up activities, such as comprehension, spelling and writing activities, should be used after reading the texts. The teacher can select from the activities in each chapter to maintain interest and variety.

While most of the chapters of the workbook present alternative spellings for vowel sounds, consonant sounds and suffixes, chapters for Books 2, 3 and 5 include activities for spellings that represent alternative sounds. These activities teach the student that he/she may need to try an alternative sound when reading certain graphemes, e.g. <c> represents 'k' in <cat> and 's' in <cell>.

An instruction for every activity in the workbook appears at the bottom of each page.

Phonic sequence in Titan's Gauntlets Series: Books 1–10

Book	Title	Phonic focus	Spellings
Book 1	An Unusual Discovery	'ue'	u, ue, u–e
Book 2	A Time for Courage	'u'	u, o, ou
Book 3	Scepter of Malice	's'	s, ss, se, c, ce
Book 4	The Coral Palace	'l'	l, ll, le, al
Book 5	Strange Energy	'j'	j, g, ge
Book 6	Phantoms of the Fog	'f'	f, ff, ph
Book 7	Unnatural Creatures	'cher'	–ture
Book 8	A Strange Location	'shun'	–tion
Book 9	Artificial Heart	'shul'	–tial, –cial
Book 10	Shattered Illusions	'zhun'	sion

Titan's Gauntlets Series Workbook

for Books 1–10

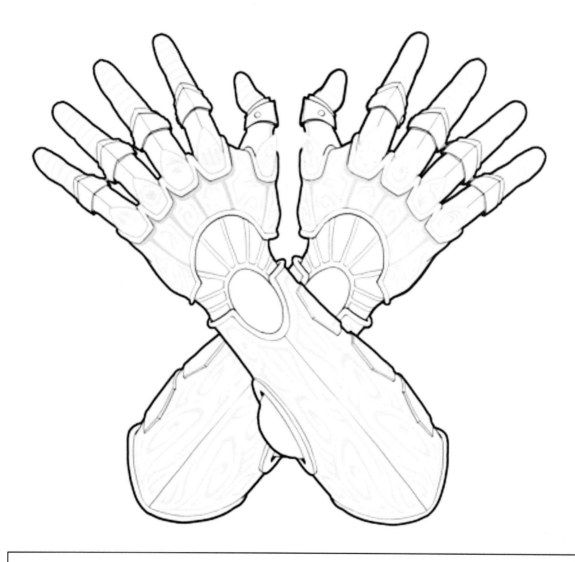

Name: _____

Students can use this page as a personalized front cover for their Titan's Gauntlets work. They may wish to decorate each finger in the gauntlet as they read the series. This sheet may be photocopied by the purchaser. © Phonic Books Ltd 2016

TITAN'S GAUNTLETS

Book 1
An Unusual Discovery

Phoneme: 'ue'
Spellings: u, ue, u–e

Book 1: Blending and segmenting 'ue'

hue	h	ue	

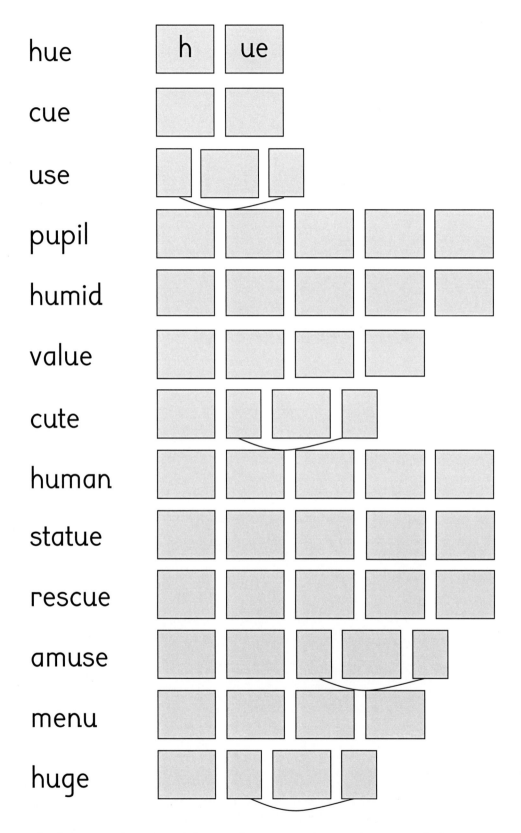

cue

use

pupil

humid

value

cute

human

statue

rescue

amuse

menu

huge

Blend the sounds and read the word. Segment the word into sounds by writing one sound in each square. Split vowel spellings (u–e) are represented by half squares linked together. This sheet may be photocopied by the purchaser. © Phonic Books Ltd 2016

Book 1: Reading and dictation 'ue'

u

human	☐
menu	☐
usual	☐
music	☐
unite	☐

u

— — — — —	☐
— — — —	☐
— — — —	☐
— — — —	☐
— — — —	☐

ue

cue	☐
hue	☐
value	☐
argue	☐
rescue	☐

ue

— —	☐
— —	☐
— — — —	☐
— — — —	☐
— — — — —	☐

u–e

cute	☐
fume	☐
cube	☐
use	☐
huge	☐

u–e

— — —	☐
— — —	☐
— — —	☐
— —	☐
— — —	☐

Fold the page along the dotted line. Ask the student to read the words on the left-hand side of the page. She/he can put a check next to them as he/she reads them. Turn over the folded page and dictate the same words to the student. He/she then opens up the page and checks his/her spelling with words in the left-hand column. This page may be photocopied by the purchaser. © Phonic Books Ltd 2016

Book 1: Reading and sorting words with 'ue' spellings

u	ue	u–e

use	cue	uniform	music
cupid	accuse	pupil	mute
human	unicorn	huge	rescue
value	cube	refuse	perfume
excuse	fume	futile	universe
useless	puny	amuse	argue
Cuba	abuse	useful	menu
mucus	statue	hue	confuse

Photocopy this page onto card and cut out the words. Read and sort the cards out according to the 'ue' headings at the top of the page. The student can highlight the spellings of 'ue' to help him/her read the words. The student can also list these words under the correct columns on the next page. This sheet may be photocopied by the purchaser. © Phonic Books Ltd 2016

Book 1: Reading and spelling 'ue'

u	ue	u-e
_____	_____	_____
_____	_____	_____
_____	_____	_____
_____	_____	_____
_____	_____	_____
_____	_____	_____
_____	_____	_____
_____	_____	_____
_____	_____	_____
_____	_____	_____
_____	_____	_____
_____	_____	_____
_____	_____	_____
_____	_____	_____
_____	_____	_____
_____	_____	_____

Write the words in the correct column according to the spelling of 'ue'. Alternatively, read Book 1 and find words with 'ue' spellings. List them in the correct columns. This sheet may be photocopied by the purchaser. © Phonic Books Ltd 2016

Book 1: Reading, sorting and spelling 'ue'

u	ue	u-e
_____	_____	_____
_____	_____	_____
_____	_____	_____
_____	_____	_____
_____	_____	_____
_____	_____	_____
_____	_____	_____
_____	_____	_____
_____	_____	_____
_____	_____	_____
_____	_____	_____

music statue use mute barbecue pupil

uniform confuse accuse cue venue humid

usual future cube amuse refuse argue value

menu universe continue excuse rescue human

useful abuse human huge perfume

Write the words in the correct column according to the spelling of 'ue'. This sheet may be photocopied by the purchaser. © Phonic Books Ltd 2016

Book 1: Cut or cute?

cut cute	hug huge	fuss fuse
us use	cub cube	mutt mute

The library was built in the shape of a _____.

A baby lion is called a _____.

Dad made a _____ when I trod mud onto the carpet.

The lights when out because the _____ had blown.

The man _____ down the trees in the forest.

My baby sister is _____.

I _____ my laptop for school work.

When it began to rain, Mrs May called _____ back into the

classroom.

Every day, Mom gives me a _____ when I leave the house.

The giant was _____.

We found a stray _____ on the street.

The video was too loud so I turned it onto '_____'.

Insert the correct words into the sentences. This sheet may be photocopied by the purchaser.
© Phonic Books Ltd 2016

Book 1: Chunking into syllables 'ue'

human _____ *hu* / *man* _____

menu _____ / _____

music _____ / _____

pupil _____ / _____

value _____ / _____

argue _____ / _____

virtue _____ / _____

rescue _____ / _____

venue _____ / _____

statue _____ / _____

useful _____ / _____

accuse _____ / _____

refuse _____ / _____

continue _____ / _____ / _____

uniform _____ / _____ / _____

usual _____ / _____ / _____

ridicule _____ / _____ / _____

Chunk the words into syllables and write the syllables on the lines. These words can also be used for dictation. This sheet may be photocopied by the purchaser. © Phonic Books Ltd 2016

Book 1: Questions for discussion

a) Why did the boat begin to sink? (pages 2, 3)

b) "It crashed into the boat and lodged there." What does the word 'lodged' mean? (page 2)

c) Why couldn't Finn paddle back to the shore? (page 3)

d) What happened to Finn after he was sucked under the water? (page 5)

e) What are gauntlets? (page 7)

f) What is special about Korus? (page 9)

g) Who is Titan? (pages 10, 11)

h) What must Finn do to help Titan regain his powers? (page 12)

i) How does Finn stop the wave from sweeping them away? (page 15)

j) What is Finn's special name? (page 16)

Book 1: What's missing in the picture?

As usual, Finn was fishing in his boat. Suddenly, the sky lit up,
streaking hues of red, yellow and orange. A rock hit the boat
and lodged in its side. Fumes rose from the rock. The boat
rocked violently and the oars fell away. Finn couldn't paddle
back to the shore. He tried to paddle with his hands. It was
useless! There was no hope of rescue.

This is a comprehension activity. Read the text carefully and draw the missing details in the picture. This sheet may be photocopied by the purchaser. © Phonic Books Ltd 2016

Book 1: Reading fluency

The current churned the waters with fury. Round and round the boat spun. The paddles were gone and there was no hope of rescue. Finn felt the sea tugging hungrily at the boat, dragging it towards a whirlpool. It was useless! There was nothing he could do to stop it! Then, he was dragged under.

Finn woke up. His head hurt. His eyes stung. The sun blazed down. What had just happened? He remembered water, water everywhere and not being able to breathe. Every tissue in his body ached and, yet, he was alive. Alive, and standing on an island!

1st reading

_____ mins

2nd reading

_____ mins

3rd reading

_____ mins

The island was unlike any Finn had seen before. Pillars and blocks of stone stood proud like statues. The stones seemed fused together. Was this an old temple or palace? The stones had strange symbols carved into them, like runes.

Suddenly, Finn saw a dazzling glint. He ran to a raised platform. There lay two unusual objects. A pair of golden gauntlets! He felt the strange holes. "Was something missing from them?" he mused. Suddenly, the gauntlets slid onto his hands as if they had a will of their own. Then, Finn had a vision. A huge warrior appeared before him.

1st reading

_____ mins

2nd reading

_____ mins

3rd reading

_____ mins

This worksheet develops reading fluency. Each text box has approximately 100 words, based on the story in the series. Fold the sheet on the dotted line. Ask the student to read the first passage three times. Each attempt is timed. In the following lesson, the teacher can ask the student to read the next passage or both passages to increase reading stamina. This sheet can be photocopied by the purchaser.
© Phonic Books Ltd 2016

Book 1: Punctuation

Capital letters and periods

Periods are needed at the end of sentences.

Capital letters are needed at the beginning of sentences and for proper nouns like names.

finn saw a dazzling glint he ran to a raised platform two unusual objects lay in front of him they were a pair of golden gauntlets he ran his fingers across the gauntlets suddenly, they slid onto his hands they seemed to have a will of their own

There are **7** capital letters and **7** periods missing.

Did you spot them all?

This is a punctuation and comprehension activity. Read the text carefully and find the missing periods and capital letters. This sheet may be photocopied by the purchaser.

Book 1: Writing activity

Dear Mom,

You'll never believe what happened to me today! I was fishing in my boat, like I do every morning, when suddenly _____

_____

_____

_____

_____

_____

_____

_____

_____

_____

Love, Finn

Ask the student to retell the story using the pictures in the book. The teacher can list the order of events to help with the sequence of the story and/or provide vocabulary to help with writing fluency. The teacher can explain the genre of letter writing, its purpose and the kind of language used in this genre. This letter is a personal letter so the language should be informal, chatty and personal. The writer can engage the audience with humor and exaggeration. This sheet may be photocopied by the purchaser. © Phonic Books Ltd 2016

Book 1: New vocabulary – cloze activity

1. **lodged** – stuck
2. **futile** – pointless
3. **majestic** – grand and impressive
4. **runes** – symbols of an ancient alphabet
5. **reduced** – made smaller or made worse
6. **mused** – gazed thoughtfully
7. **dismissed** – sent away

Finn lay in the boat and gazed up at the blue sky. "Shall I collect crabs?" he _____. "No!" He quickly _____ the idea. Suddenly, the sky lit up and a rock struck his boat. It was _____ in the boat. The boat rocked and the paddles fell into the water. Finn tried to paddle with his hands, but it was _____.

Soon he was sucked under! Next, he found himself on an island. There were blocks of stone and strange _____ carved into them. Suddenly, he saw a glint. There lay a pair of golden gauntlets. They were _____. Then he met Korus, the songbird of the seas. Korus explained that Titan had power once, but it was _____ by the evil Winged One.

Read and discuss new words with the student. Offer an example sentence with the new words if needed. The student can then give an example sentence. Ask the student to read the text and fill in the missing words and then reread the passage with the new vocabulary inserted in the text. This sheet may be photocopied by the purchaser. © Phonic Books Ltd 2016

Book 1: Comprehension – True or false?

Prometheus, the Titan

Prometheus chained to a rock

The Titans were the first gods in Greek mythology. They came before Zeus and the Olympian Gods. There was a mighty battle between Zeus and the Titans and, in the end, Zeus won.

Prometheus was one of the Titans. He was given the task of creating man. He made man out of mud. The Goddess Athena breathed life into his clay figure.

Prometheus loved man and wanted to help him. He tricked Zeus by offering him a sacrifice that looked juicy but actually had only bones inside. He gave the good, nourishing meat to man. Zeus got angry and took fire away from man. Prometheus stole the fire and gave it back to man. Zeus was so enraged that he punished Prometheus by chaining him to a rock. An eagle pecked at his liver by day and it would grow back every night.

The Greeks believed that Prometheus gave man writing, mathematics, agriculture, medicine and science.

Is it true?   **yes**   **no**

Titans were gods who came before Zeus.   ☐   ☐

Prometheus had the task of creating animals.   ☐   ☐

He made man out of straw.   ☐   ☐

Zeus and Prometheus were friends.   ☐   ☐

Prometheus stole fire and gave it to man.   ☐   ☐

An eagle pecked his head every day.   ☐   ☐

Book 1: Comprehension quiz

Write the correct answer on the line.

1. Finn was in his _____ when the skyshard hit it.
a) bike   b) book   c) boat   d) bench

2. Finn was sucked underwater and then emerged onto an _____.
a) river   b) volcano   c) valley   d) island

3. He found a pair of magical _____.
a) helmets   b) boots   c) gauntlets   d) bracelets

4. Korus was Titan's _____.
a) messenger   b) teacher   c) singer   d) gardener

5. Finn had to find the skyshards and insert them into the
_____.
a) hat   b) pockets   c) gauntlets   d) trousers

6. Finn stopped the huge wave by making an ice _____.
a) cream   b) ramp   c) wall   d) lake

7. When Finn used the gauntlets, Korus was _____.
a) sad   b) grumpy   c) happy   d) astonished

8. Finn couldn't believe he was the _____ one.
a) frozen   b) broken   c) chosen   d) sleepy

Book 1: Spelling assessment

1.

ue	**u**	**u-e**
rescue	music	use
value	pupil	cube
statue	human	huge
argue	unit	cute

2.

ue	**u**	**u-e**
venue	uniform	refuse
avenue	cucumber	excuse
continue	funeral	accuse
	document	amuse
	unicorn	ridicule

This list can be used as a spelling assessment at the end of each unit of work. The teacher can add words from list 2 for able students. When dictating a word, say the word. Then say a sentence with the word in it (to put the word in the context of a sentence) and then repeat the word. E.g. "Rescue. I had to rescue the dog from the pond. Rescue." This ensures that the student has heard the word correctly. This sheet may be photocopied by the purchaser.

Book 1 – Line-up game 'ue'

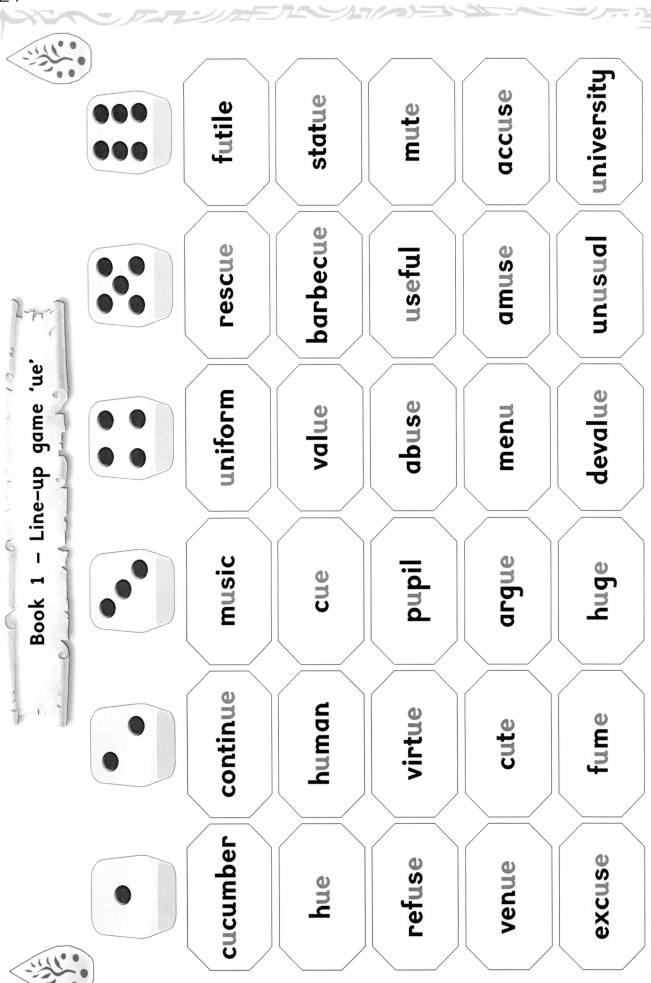

●	●●	●●●	●●●●	●●●●●	●●●●●●
cucumber	continue	music	uniform	rescue	futile
hue	human	cue	value	barbecue	statue
refuse	virtue	pupil	abuse	useful	mute
venue	cute	argue	menu	amuse	accuse
excuse	fume	huge	devalue	unusual	university

This game is for two players. Each player needs a batch of counters of one color. The players take turns to throw the die. They read a word in the column that corresponds to the number on the die and place their counter on that word. The first to have three of his/her counters in a row is the winner.

TITAN'S GAUNTLETS

Book 2
A Time for Courage

Phoneme: 'u'
Spellings: u, o, ou

Book 2: Blending and segmenting 'u'

gull	g	u	ll		
ton					
tough					
pump					
some					
come					
young					
enough					
month					
Monday					
cousin					
nothing					
trouble					

Blend the sounds and read the word. Segment the word into sounds by writing one sound in each square. This sheet may be photocopied by the purchaser. © Phonic Books Ltd 2016

27

Book 2: Reading and dictation 'u'

u

sun	☐
dull	☐
bulk	☐
pluck	☐
scrunch	☐

u

____	☐
_____	☐
_____	☐
_____	☐
_____	☐

o

son	☐
come	☐
some	☐
month	☐
Monday	☐

o

____	☐
_____	☐
_____	☐
_____	☐
_____	☐

ou

young	☐
touch	☐
cousin	☐
double	☐
enough	☐

ou

_____	☐
_____	☐
_____	☐
_____	☐
_____	☐

Fold the page along the dotted line. Ask the student to read the words on the left-hand side of the page. She/he can put a check next to them as he/she reads them. Turn over the folded page and dictate the same words to the student. He/she then opens up the page and checks his/her spelling with words in the left-hand column. This page may be photocopied by the purchaser. © Phonic Books Ltd 2016

Book 2: Reading and sorting words with 'u' spellings

u	o	ou

tough	other	brother	gulf
money	come	stun	enough
worry	nourish	dozen	courage
another	mother	double	nothing
pulp	son	rough	couple
sun	monkey	plush	touch
above	among	love	oven
hurry	trouble	front	ton

Photocopy this page onto card and cut out the words. Read and sort the cards out according to the 'u' headings at the top of the page. The student can highlight the spellings of 'u' to help him/her read the words. The student can also list these words under the correct columns on the next page. This sheet may be photocopied by the purchaser.

Book 2: Reading and spelling 'u'

u	o	ou
_____	_____	_____
_____	_____	_____
_____	_____	_____
_____	_____	_____
_____	_____	_____
_____	_____	_____
_____	_____	_____
_____	_____	_____
_____	_____	_____
_____	_____	_____
_____	_____	_____
_____	_____	_____
_____	_____	_____
_____	_____	_____
_____	_____	_____
_____	_____	_____

Write the words in the correct column according to the spelling of 'u'. This sheet may be photocopied by the purchaser. © Phonic Books Ltd 2016

Book 2: Reading, sorting and spelling 'u'

u	o	ou
_____	_____	_____
_____	_____	_____
_____	_____	_____
_____	_____	_____
_____	_____	_____
_____	_____	_____
_____	_____	_____
_____	_____	_____
_____	_____	_____
_____	_____	_____

gull   some   touch   love   mother   plug   above

come   couple   son   rush   ton   cousin   worry

wonder   tough   stuff   enough   another

nourish   money   front   double   trouble   sulk

young   brother   above   dozen   courage

Write the words in the correct column according to the spelling of 'u'. This sheet may be photocopied by the purchaser. © Phonic Books Ltd 2016

Book 2: Chunking into syllables: 'u'

cousin _____ / _____

handcuff _____ / _____

monkey _____ / _____

roughly _____ / _____

uncle _____ / _____

courage _____ / _____

southern _____ / _____

enough _____ / _____

nourish _____ / _____

stunning _____ / _____

brother _____ / _____

mother _____ / _____

country _____ / _____

nothing _____ / _____

encourage _____ / _____ / _____

government _____ / _____ / _____

worrisome _____ / _____ / _____

Chunk the words into syllables and write the syllables on the lines. These words can also be used for dictation. This sheet may be photocopied by the purchaser. © Phonic Books Ltd 2016

Book 2: Reading and sorting words with <ou> spelling

you	touch	out

group	rough	about	route
pound	soup	young	sound
coupon	enough	mouse	courage
cloud	trouble	ghoul	hound
cousin	southern	count	house
double	tough	noun	found
ground	country	ounce	nourish

Photocopy this page onto card and cut out the words. Read and sort the cards out according to sounds of the <ou> spelling. The three sounds are: 'oo', 'u' and 'ow'. This sheet can also be used as a timed reading activity. This sheet may be photocopied by the purchaser. © Phonic Books Ltd 2016

Book 2: Questions for discussion

a) Why is Titan moving? (page 2)

b) How will Finn know where to find the next skyshard? (page 3)

c) What does the skyshard in the gauntlet tell Finn? (page 5)

d) Where is the next skyshard hidden? (page 5)

e) What must Finn do to reach the next skyshard? (page 7)

f) Why must Korus distract the dreadsnakes? (page 9)

g) Why did Finn freeze with terror when he was up the pillar?

   (page 11)

h) How does Finn trap the dreadsnakes? (page 12)

i) What does Finn do with the skyshard when he reaches it?

   (page 13)

j) How does Finn get down from the pillar? (pages 15, 16)

Book 2: What's missing in the picture?

Tough weeds had taken root on the pillar. Finn grasped hold of

them. In a heartbeat, dozens of branches grew, green leaves

blooming from their tips. A maze of branches had sprouted

around the dreadsnakes. Trapped between the crooked

branches, they squirmed and snapped their jaws. Finn was

safe!

This is a comprehension activity. Read the text carefully and draw the missing details in the picture. This sheet may be photocopied by the purchaser. © Phonic Books Ltd 2016

Book 2: Reading fluency

Just then, something caught Finn's eye. A swarm of dark shapes flew among the pillars.
"Dreadsnakes! Servants of our enemy!" spat Korus.
"They will try and stop us! We must get the shard quickly!"

Titan pulled up beside the pillar with the skyshard on it.
"Go, Chosen One! If the dreadsnakes come, I will distract them!" Finn jumped onto the pillar. He touched the barnacles and shells.

"Can I use them to climb the pillar?" he wondered.
Finn looked up above. He had a long way to climb.
He pulled himself up, one shell after another.

1st reading	_____ mins
2nd reading	_____ mins
3rd reading	_____ mins

- -

Soon Finn was dripping with sweat. His arms were shaking. He tightened his grip on the rough surface.
He looked down at the sheer drop. He felt vertigo.
Finn gulped. He began to worry. Would he make it to the top?
"Kraaa!" Deafening shrieks came from above.
Suddenly, a horde of dreadsnakes came straight at him. Sharp fangs hung like needles from gaping mouths. In a flash, Korus appeared by his side. The dreadsnakes turned to chase him.
"Courage, Finn!" he called.
"Courage!" Finn repeated and urged himself to climb faster.

1st reading	_____ mins
2nd reading	_____ mins
3rd reading	_____ mins

This worksheet develops reading fluency. Each text box has approximately 100 words, based on the story in the series. Fold the sheet on the dotted line. Ask the student to read the first passage three times. Each attempt is timed. In the following lesson, the teacher can ask the student to read the next passage or both passages to increase reading stamina. This sheet can be photocopied by the purchaser.
© Phonic Books Ltd 2016

Book 2: Punctuation

Capital letters and periods

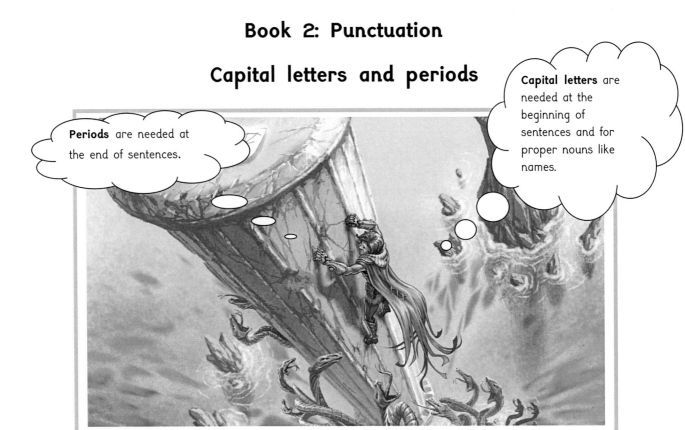

finn gritted his teeth and hauled himself upwards he clambered up like a gecko he could see the shining shard it was on top of the pillar suddenly, he heard the troubling shrieks of the dreadsnakes a dozen dreadsnakes were coming right at him

There are **6** capital letters and **6** periods missing.

Did you spot them all?

Book 2: Writing activity

Dear Mom,

Did I tell you that I am chosen to help the giant Titan regain his powers? This Titan is actually an island and guess what? It moves! We set off to the west and soon we came to the strangest place! It looked like

_____

_____

_____

_____

_____

_____

_____

_____

Ask the student to retell the story using the pictures in the book. The teacher can list the order of events to help with the sequence of the story and/or provide vocabulary to help with writing fluency. The teacher can explain the genre of letter writing, its purpose and the kind of language used in this genre. This letter is a personal letter so the language should be informal, chatty and personal. The writer can engage the audience with humor and exaggeration. This sheet may be photocopied by the purchaser. © Phonic Books Ltd 2016

Book 2: New vocabulary – cloze activity

1. **among** – in between
2. **clambered** – climbed with hands and feet awkwardly
3. **shudder** – a shake
4. **scattered** – thrown in different directions
5. **barnacles** – seashells that latch onto ships and rocks
6. **etched** – carved into something
7. **jolt** – a sudden rough shake or jerk

Finn woke up with a _____. The ground beneath him

began to _____. He realized that Titan was moving! Korus

explained that the skyshards had been _____ across the

ocean. Finn had to find them and insert them into the gauntlets.

Finn looked at the _____ symbols in the gauntlets. He

saw a circle and some kind of vine. What could it be? Soon they

came to a circle of pillars. Finn could see the skyshard glinting

from the top of one of the pillars. Suddenly, a swarm of

dreadsnakes flew _____ the pillars. He _____ up

the pillars as fast as he could. He clung onto the _____

and pulled himself up.

Book 2: Comprehension – True or false?

The Greek Myth of King Ceyx and Halcyon

> The character of Korus in 'Titan's Gauntlets' was inspired by a kingfisher.

Zeus sends a storm to kill King Ceyx

A kingfisher bird

King Ceyx and his wife, Halcyon, were happily married. They were so in love that they used to joke and call each other 'Zeus' and 'Hera'. This angered Zeus, the god, who thought it was disrespectful and he decided to punish King Ceyx.

One day, King Ceyx decided to travel the seas to consult the Oracle of Apollo. (The Oracle of Apollo was a priestess who gave messages to humans from the god Apollo.) This was Zeus's opportunity to punish King Ceyx. He struck King Ceyx's ship with a thunderbolt. King Ceyx drowned in the storm. Poor Halcyon found his body washed up on the shore. She was so distraught, she couldn't live without him. She threw herself into the waters and drowned herself. When the gods saw this, they felt sorry for Halcyon and King Ceyx. They thought the punishment was unjust. Zeus felt bad, so he changed them into kingfisher birds.

According to the legend, every January, there are fourteen days when the wind and waves calm down. This allows the kingfisher bird to dig a nest in the sand and lay her eggs in peace. Today, the phrase 'Halcyon days' means a short time of peace and quiet.

Is it true?	yes	no
Halcyon and King Ceyx called each other by gods' names.	☐	☐
Zeus thought they didn't respect him enough.	☐	☐
Zeus was a kind god.	☐	☐
Halcyon drowned because she was unhappy with King Ceyx.	☐	☐
The gods were happy that Halcyon and King Ceyx had died.	☐	☐
'Halcyon days' means a short time of peace.	☐	☐

Read the text. Now read the sentences above and put a cross in the boxes according to whether they are true or false. This sheet may be photocopied by the purchaser. © Phonic Books Ltd 2016

Book 2: Comprehension quiz

Write the correct answer on the line.

1. Finn found out that Titan was _____.
   a) jumping   b) running   c) moving   d) chatting

2. Finn looked at the skyshard to find the next _____.
   a) fish   b) blanket   c) river   d) clue

3. The symbol on the skyshard was a circle and a kind of _____.
   a) vine   b) rock   c) cloud   d) rain

4. The next skyshard was at the top of a _____.
   a) wall   b) mountain   c) hill   d) pillar

5. Finn was attacked by _____.
   a) lizards   b) bees   c) dreadsnakes   d) spiders

6. Finn held on to _____ as he climbed up.
   a) snails   b) barnacles   c) branches   d) windows

7. Finn touched the branches and they began to _____.
   a) sprout   b) fall   c) crack   d) wilt

8. Finn grabbed a _____ as he plummeted down.
   a) stick   b) branch   c) leaf   d) dreadsnake

Book 2: Spelling assessment

1.

<u>u</u>	<u>ou</u>	<u>o</u>
under	young	come
until	touch	some
ugly	cousin	month
sum	country	Monday

- -

2.

<u>u</u>	<u>ou</u>	<u>o</u>
sun	double	son
plump	courage	nothing
thumb	tough	other
		mother
		brother

This list can be used as a spelling assessment at the end of each unit of work. The teacher can add words from list 2 for able students. When dictating a word, say the word. Then say a sentence with the word in it (to put the word in the context of a sentence) and then repeat the word. E.g. "Rescue. I had to rescue the dog from the pond. Rescue." This ensures that the student has heard the word correctly. The teacher can include homophones, e.g. 'sum/some' but will need to explain them to the student. This sheet may be photocopied by the purchaser.

Book 2 – Line-up game 'u'

1	2	3	4	5	6
fun	young	enough	sunk	double	couple
love	slump	ton	come	cousin	mother
touch	brother	rough	dump	tough	trouble
flung	son	trumpet	glum	other	nothing
above	pluck	country	hunt	courage	some

This game is for two players. Each player needs a batch of counters of one color. The players take turns to throw the die. They read a word in the column that corresponds to the number on the die and place their counter on that word. The first to have three of his/her counters in a row is the winner.

TITAN'S GAUNTLETS

Book 3
Scepter of Malice

Phoneme: 's'
Spellings: s, ss, se, c, ce

Book 3: Blending and segmenting: 's'

sell	s	e	ll		
mess					
rinse					
cell					
choice					
slump						
dress					
house					
circle					
piece					
tense					
balance						
certain					

Blend the sounds and read the word. Segment the word into sounds by writing one sound in each square. This sheet may be photocopied by the purchaser. © Phonic Books Ltd 2016

Book 3: Reading and dictation 's'

se

rinse	☐
tense	☐
pulse	☐
mouse	☐
horse	☐

se

— — — — —	☐
— — — —	☐
— — — —	☐
— — —	☐
— — —	☐

c

cell	☐
cent	☐
cycle	☐
cement	☐
circle	☐

c

— — — —	☐
— — —	☐
— — — —	☐
— — — — — —	☐
— — — — —	☐

ce

fence	☐
wince	☐
voice	☐
choice	☐
chance	☐

ce

— — — — —	☐
— — — —	☐
— — —	☐
— — — —	☐
— — — —	☐

Fold the page along the dotted line. Ask the student to read the words on the left-hand side of the page. She/he can put a check next to them as he/she reads them. Turn over the folded page and dictate the same words to the student. He/she then opens up the page and checks his/her spelling with words in the left-hand column. This page may be photocopied by the purchaser. © Phonic Books Ltd 2016

Book 3: Reading and sorting words with 's' spellings

s	ss	se	c	ce

still	press	certain	dance
peace	since	worse	cycle
voice	cell	mouse	dense
fence	century	sense	police
circle	piece	cent	presence
bounce	balance	purse	ceiling
horse	center	tense	cellar
stand	distress	fleece	floss

Photocopy this page onto card and cut out the words. Read and sort the cards out according to the 's' headings at the top of the page. The student can highlight the spellings of 's' to help him/her read the words. The student can also list these words under the correct columns on the next page. This sheet may be photocopied by the purchaser. © Phonic Books Ltd 2016

Book 3: Reading and spelling 's'

s	ss	se
____	____	____
____	____	____
____	____	____
____	____	____
____	____	____
____	____	____
____	____	____

c	ce
____	____
____	____
____	____
____	____
____	____
____	____
____	____

Write the words in the correct column according to the spelling of 's'. This sheet may be photocopied by the purchaser. © Phonic Books Ltd 2016

Book 3: Reading, sorting and spelling 's'

s	ss	se
_____	_____	_____
_____	_____	_____
_____	_____	_____
_____	_____	_____
_____	_____	_____
_____	_____	_____

c	ce
_____	_____
_____	_____
_____	_____
_____	_____
_____	_____

press   sink   cement   tense   star   mouse

fence   moss   rinse   circle   mince   safe   guess

notice   pulse   excel   celebrate   sort   blossom

string   possible   certain   juice   cycle   worse

horse   distress   chance   peace   slump

Write the words in the correct column according to the spelling of 's'. This sheet may be photocopied by the purchaser. © Phonic Books Ltd 2016

Book 3: Chunking into syllables: 's'

stressful _____/_____

unless _____/_____

densely _____/_____

circle _____/_____

center _____/_____

advance _____/_____

distress _____/_____

falsely _____/_____

accept _____/_____

sentence _____/_____

presence _____/_____

racing _____/_____

succeed _____/_____

silence _____/_____

possible _____/_____/_____

celebrate _____/_____/_____

century _____/_____/_____

Chunk the words into syllables and write the syllables on the lines. These words can also be used for dictation. This sheet may be photocopied by the purchaser. © Phonic Books Ltd 2016

Book 3: Reading and sorting words with <c> spelling

cat	cent

crust	civil	clap	cycle
circle	center	focus	certain
ceiling	care	cement	census
cloud	celebrate	cold	cell
crisp	cigar	uncle	century
castle	ceramic	celebrity	cedar

Photocopy this page onto card and cut out the words. Read and sort the cards out according to sounds of the <c> spelling. The two sounds are: 'k' and 's'. This sheet can also be used as a timed reading activity. This sheet may be photocopied by the purchaser.

Book 3: Questions for discussion

a) Why does Finn call Korus 'bird brains'? (page 2)

b) What is the clue on the second skyshard? (page 3)

c) What did the spider's web actually turn out to be? (page 4)

d) Who shot arrows at Finn and Korus? (page 8)

e) Where was the skyshard hidden? (page 8)

f) Why does Finn speak meekly to the menacing men? (page 9)

g) Why do the men want to capture Korus? (page 10)

h) How does Finn stop the arrows from raining down on them again? (page 12)

i) How do Finn and Korus get the skyshard from the scepter? (page 14)

j) Why does Korus say, "I can get a good price for him!"? (page 16)

Book 3: What's missing in the picture?

On the bridge above them stood a band of menacing-looking men holding bows and arrows. One of the men stepped forward and spat into the water. He held the skyshard in a scepter.

"I don't remember inviting you to this gathering!" he growled with malice.

Book 3: Reading fluency

From a distance, Finn and Korus spotted some small islands. As they came closer, they saw the islands were linked by rope bridges. Titan glided silently beneath them.

"Just like a spider's web," said Finn in a hushed voice. The islands seemed abandoned. A rope dangled from one bridge. Finn could not resist it.

"Time to try my excellent circus skills!" he yelled to Korus, swinging on the rope.

There was a loud splash as Finn lost his grip and dropped into the sea. Korus looked on and grinned. Dripping wet and embarrassed, Finn clambered back onto Titan.

| 1st reading |
| _____ mins |

| 2nd reading |
| _____ mins |

| 3rd reading |
| _____ mins |

Finn spotted a glint of light coming from one of the bridges.

"Look! I think I see a skyshard!" he called, but Korus was concentrating on something else.

"I am listening to the sea," said Korus, "It says we are in danger!"

Just then, a hail of arrows rained down. Korus and Finn threw themselves to the ground. The attack was short but intense. Then, there was an eerie silence. Korus glanced up and squawked. On the bridge above them stood a band of menacing-looking men holding bows and arrows. One of the men stepped forward and spat into the water.

| 1st reading |
| _____ mins |

| 2nd reading |
| _____ mins |

| 3rd reading |
| _____ mins |

This worksheet develops reading fluency. Each text box has approximately 100 words, based on the story in the series. Fold the sheet on the dotted line. Ask the student to read the first passage three times. Each attempt is timed. In the following lesson, the teacher can ask the student to read the next passage or both passages to increase reading stamina. This sheet can be photocopied by the purchaser.
© Phonic Books Ltd 2016

Book 3: Punctuation

Capital letters, periods and question marks

Periods are needed at the end of sentences.

Question marks are needed at the end of sentences that are questions.

Capital letters are needed at the beginning of sentences and for proper nouns like names.

finn gazed around him at the still waters where would the next skyshard be

he held the gauntlets up and traced the symbol on the last skyshard it seemed to be a spider's web where would a spider's web be on the ocean finn could no make sense of it

There are **6** capital letters, **4** periods and **2** question marks missing. Did you spot them all?

This is a punctuation and comprehension activity. Read the text carefully and find the missing periods, capital letters and question marks. This sheet may be photocopied by the purchaser.
© Phonic Books Ltd 2016

Book 3: Writing activity

My favorite part so far

My favorite book in the series so far is book
number _____ because

_____

_____

_____

_____

_____

My favorite page so far is page _____ because

_____

_____

_____

_____

Discuss Books 1–3 in the series and ask the student to choose his/her favorite book and to explain why he/she has chosen that book. Ask the student to find his/her favorite illustration and to explain what he/she likes about it. This sheet may be photocopied by the purchaser. © Phonic Books Ltd 2016

Book 3: New vocabulary – cloze activity

1. **resist** – to stop oneself from doing something
2. **traced** – followed a pattern with his hand
3. **dismay** – unhappiness about something that has happened
4. **abandoned** – left or deserted
5. **eerie** – strange and frightening
6. **winced** – pulled a face
7. **retorted** – answered in a sharp, angry way

Korus swooped down into the sea and caught a fish. Finn

_____. "You eat so much! Are you sure you're not a pig?"

"How can I be a pig when I have feathers?" Korus _____.

Finn slapped his forehead in _____. Then he gazed at the

gauntlets. He _____ the symbol of the last shard with his

finger.

Soon they came to some islands. They seemed _____.

Finn saw a rope hanging from one of the bridges. He could not

_____ jumping up and swinging on it. He lost his grip and

splashed into the sea. Then, there was an _____ silence.

Book 3: Comprehension – True or false?

Atlas, the Titan

Atlas was one of the Titans who came before the Olympian gods in Greek mythology. Zeus was an Olympian god and he fought the Titans. He defeated them and locked them up in a dungeon called Tartarus. This is where the evil and wicked were locked up.

Zeus gave Atlas a special punishment. He had to hold up the heavens for eternity. Atlas is always shown in Greek sculptures as holding up the heavens. He did not like this punishment. It was hard work and very boring.

Now, Heracules had to bring Zeus some golden apples. The apple orchard was guarded by the dragon Ladon, who had one hundred heads.

Heracles asked Atlas to help him get the apples. Atlas agreed to help. This was his chance to trick Heracles and change places with him. He asked Heracles to take his place and hold up the heavens while he, Atlas, fetched the apples. Atlas managed to get the apples and offered to deliver the apples to Zeus himself. He knew that anyone who purposely took on the job of holding up the heavens would have to do it forever. Heracles suspected that Atlas wanted to trick him. He asked Atlas to hold the heavens for a few minutes while he rearranged his cloak to make better padding on his shoulders. Heracles took the apples and ran away!

Is it true?

	yes	no
Zeus locked Atlas in a dungeon.	☐	☐
Altas had to hold up the heavens for one year.	☐	☐
Altas liked holding up the heavens.	☐	☐
The golden apples were in a garden guarded by a dragon.	☐	☐
Atlas wanted Heracles to take his place.	☐	☐
Heracles suspected the trick and tricked Atlas instead.	☐	☐

Read the text. Now read the sentences below and put a cross in the boxes according to whether they are true or false. This sheet may be photocopied by the purchaser. © Phonic Books Ltd 2016

Book 3: Comprehension quiz

Write the correct answer on the line.

1. Titan drifted towards a group of _____.
a) towers   b) islands   c) castles   d) mountains

2. The islands were linked by _____.
a) planks   b) tunnels   c) threads   d) rope bridges

3. Finn grabbed a dangling _____.
a) tree   b) cloth   c) rope   d) belt

4. Finn and Korus were attacked by a hail of _____.
a) arrows   b) knives   c) spears   d) daggers

5. The skyshard was embedded in a _____.
a) shield   b) cloak   c) crown   d) scepter

6. The word 'meekly' means being _____.
a) aggressively   b) gently   c) happy   d) silly

7. The word 'menacing' means _____.
a) pretending   b) happening   c) threatening   d) boring

8. The band of men fell from the bridge into the _____.
a) river   b) pit   c) grass   d) sea

Book 3: Spelling assessment

s	**ss**	**se**
self	dress	house
sad	class	mouse
risk	guess	horse
seen	press	sense

ce	**c**
once	circle
place	cycle
nice	December
twice	pencil

This list can be used as a spelling assessment at the end of each unit of work. The teacher can add words from list 2 for able students. When dictating a word, say the word. Then say a sentence with the word in it (to put the word in the context of a sentence) and then repeat the word. E.g. "Rescue. I had to rescue the dog from the pond. Rescue." This ensures that the student has heard the word correctly. This sheet may be photocopied by the purchaser.

Book 3 – Line-up game 's'

	cellar	false	miss	slip	tense	list
	mouse	notice	jets	rinse	cycle	distress
	fossil	accept	pulse	since	possible	worse
	excel	receive	course	guess	century	voice
	entrance	horse	dance	circle	fence	cement

This game is for two players. Each player needs a batch of counters of one color. The players take turns to throw the die. They read a word in the column that corresponds to the number on the die and place their counter on that word. The first to have three of his/her counters in a row is the winner.

This sheet may be photocopied by the purchaser. © Phonic Books 2016

TITAN'S GAUNTLETS

Book 4
The Coral Palace

Phoneme: 'l'
Spellings: l, ll, le, al

Book 4: Blending and segmenting: 'l'

long	l	o	ng			
chill						
hassle						
medal						
glass						
drill						
trample						
final						
grumble						
crystal						
total						
signal						
central						

Blend the sounds and read the word. Segment the word into sounds by writing one sound in each square. This sheet may be photocopied by the purchaser. © Phonic Books Ltd 2016

Book 4: Reading and dictation 'l'

l and ll

last	☐
self	☐
bill	☐
grill	☐
still	☐

le

paddle	☐
middle	☐
handle	☐
jungle	☐
ankle	☐

al

medal	☐
final	☐
signal	☐
total	☐
animal	☐

l and ll

(blank dictation lines)

le

(blank dictation lines)

al

(blank dictation lines)

Fold the page along the dotted line. Ask the student to read the words on the left-hand side of the page. She/he can put a check next to them as he/she reads them. Turn over the folded page and dictate the same words to the student. He/she then opens up the page and checks his/her spelling with words in the left-hand column. This page may be photocopied by the purchaser. © Phonic Books Ltd 2016

Book 4: Reading and sorting words with 'l' spellings

l	ll	le	al

still	lost	riddle	fable
animal	brilliant	temple	central
medal	stumble	refill	total
plastic	coral	crystal	musical
simple	helpful	pull	final
length	huddle	critical	trifle
needle	shrill	full	gobble
stable	miracle	link	cradle

Photocopy this page onto card and cut out the words. Read and sort the cards out according to the 'l' headings at the top of the page. The student can highlight the spellings of 'l' to help him/her read the words. The student can also list these words under the correct columns on the next page. This sheet may be photocopied by the purchaser. © Phonic Books Ltd 2016

Book 4: Reading and spelling 'l'

l	ll
_____	_____
_____	_____
_____	_____
_____	_____
_____	_____
_____	_____
_____	_____

le	al
_____	_____
_____	_____
_____	_____
_____	_____
_____	_____
_____	_____
_____	_____
_____	_____
_____	_____

Write the words in the correct column according to the spelling of 'l'. This sheet may be photocopied by the purchaser. © Phonic Books Ltd 2016

Book 4: Reading, sorting and spelling 'l'

l	le	al
___	___	___
___	___	___
___	___	___
___	___	___
___	___	___

ll

___	___	___
___	___	___
___	___	___
___	___	___

call   limp   middle   central   petal   gobble   angle

refill   hassle   simple   medal   legal   plump   brilliant

little   usual   total   handle   ankle   puddle

signal   coastal   critical   spill   loose   mortal

mystical   animal   temple   jungle   diagonal

Write the words in the correct column according to the spelling of 'l'. This sheet may be photocopied by the purchaser. © Phonic Books Ltd 2016

Book 4: Chunking into syllables: 'l'

table   _____ / _____

little   _____ / _____

trifle   _____ / _____

landed   _____ / _____

pedal   _____ / _____

mortal   _____ / _____

trickle   _____ / _____

final   _____ / _____

noble   _____ / _____

drilling   _____ / _____

central   _____ / _____

mental   _____ / _____

cuddle   _____ / _____

pickle   _____ / _____

animal   _____ / _____ / _____

minimal   _____ / _____ / _____

usual   _____ / _____ / _____

Chunk the words into syllables and write the syllables on the lines. These words can also be used for dictation. This sheet may be photocopied by the purchaser. © Phonic Books Ltd 2016

Book 4: Questions for discussion

a) Why does Finn shudder? (page 1)

b) What does the word 'regal' mean? (page 3)

c) What happened to the Coral Queen's kingdom? (page 4)

d) How did Finn manage to stay underwater for so long? (page 7)

e) Finn did not relish the idea of diving underwater. What does

that mean? (page 8)

f) Why were there no fish underwater? (page 10)

g) Why does Finn think the kingdom is a 'watery grave'? (page 10)

h) The tendrils coiled around Finn's body. What does that mean?

(page 12)

i) How did Finn free himself from the tendrils? (page 13)

j) How did Finn know that the underwater kingdom was coming

back to life? (page 14)

Book 4: What's missing in the picture?

Finn needed to find the skyshard and free it from this watery

grave. He swam until he reached a grand underwater chamber.

There, in the middle, shone a bright skyshard. He reached out

for it. All of a sudden, tendrils of black seaweed burst from the

coral. One tendril grasped his ankle. It wound itself round and

round his leg.

This is a comprehension activity. Read the text carefully and draw the missing details in the picture. This sheet may be photocopied by the purchaser. © Phonic Books Ltd 2016

Book 4: Reading fluency

Finn plunged into the water. He did not relish the idea of being underwater, but he wanted to help the Coral Queen. Down he dived until he came to the home of the Coral Queen. It was a magical place! Each structure was made of coral, twisted into different forms.

Then Finn noticed something odd: there were no fish swimming around, none at all! The Coral Queen was right. Her kingdom was covered in terrible black seaweed. Tendrils curled around everything like coiled slippery snakes. They had strangled the life from the Coral Kingdom. Finn needed to find the skyshard.

1st reading
_____ mins

2nd reading
_____ mins

3rd reading
_____ mins

Finn swam on and reached a grand underwater chamber. There, in the middle, shone a bright skyshard. He reached out for it.

All of a sudden, tendrils of black seaweed burst from the coral. One tendril grasped his ankle. It wound itself round and round his leg. Finn tried to rip it off. He grappled and wrestled with it, but it was no use! More tendrils were coming! They coiled around his body. Tighter and tighter, the terrible tendrils crushed him. Even with the bubble, he could hardly breathe. Finn began to feel faint. He desperately needed air. It was critical!

1st reading
_____ mins

2nd reading
_____ mins

3rd reading
_____ mins

This worksheet develops reading fluency. Each text box has approximately 100 words, based on the story in the series. Fold the sheet on the dotted line. Ask the student to read the first passage three times. Each attempt is timed. In the following lesson, the teacher can ask the student to read the next passage or both passages to increase reading stamina. This sheet can be photocopied by the purchaser.

Book 4: Punctuation

Capital letters, periods and question marks

Periods are needed at the end of sentences.

Question marks are needed at the end of sentences that are questions.

Capital letters are needed at the beginning of sentences and for proper nouns like names.

finn began to feel faint he needed air
could the skyshard help him
he reached up above him all at once, jets of
steam burst from the gauntlets and helped him
blast away from the seaweed

There are **5** capital letters, **4** periods and **1** question mark missing. Did you spot them all?

This is a punctuation and comprehension activity. Read the text carefully and find the missing periods, capital letters and question marks. This sheet may be photocopied by the purchaser.
© Phonic Books Ltd 2016

Book 4: Writing activity – similes

Write the most suitable simile on the line.

| desert | shivering leaf | daggers | killer whale |

Titan surged through the ocean **as fast as a** _____.

Here and there, jagged rocks broke the surface **like** _____.

Suddenly, Finn and Korus heard a shrill voice call "Excuse me!" The

voice trembled **like a** _____. "Deadly seaweed has

destroyed my kingdom. It is **like a** _____."

Now write your own similes on the lines.

Finn plunged into the water. Down and down he dived **like a**

_____. The sea was **as** cold **as** _____.

He saw the magical kingdom of the Coral Queen. He spotted the

skyshard. It glinted **like a** _____. Suddenly, the black

tendrils grasped his leg. They coiled around his body **as tight as**

a _____.

A simile is a comparison of a thing with something different. It is used to paint a picture in the mind of the reader. When writing a simile, the words 'as (cold) as' or 'like' are used for this comparison. Explain similes to the student, give some examples, e.g. 'as black as night'. Ask the student to invent some imaginative examples. This sheet may be photocopied by the purchaser.

Book 4: New vocabulary – cloze activity

1. **engulfed** – surrounded on all sides
2. **chamber** – a room
3. **churning** – shaking or turning over (of a liquid)
4. **regal** – like a king or queen
5. **did not relish** – did not look forward to
6. **marooned** – abandoned on an island
7. **tendrils** – threadlike parts of a plant that attach themselves to nearby objects in order to grow

Finn looked at the waters below. They were _____.

Suddenly he heard a shrill voice. There was a _____ old

woman. She was _____ on some rocks. The Coral Queen

explained that her kingdom had been invaded by deadly ocean

weeds. She told Finn about a jewel that was down below in her

kingdom. Korus sang to the seas. A big bubble _____ Finn's

head. Now he could breathe underwater! Finn feared the depths of

the sea and did not _____ the idea of being deep

underwater. He plunged in. Soon he came to a magical kingdom.

It was covered in black, slippery _____. He swam until he

reached an underwater _____.

Book 4: Comprehension – True or false?

Corals

Coral reefs are found in clear, tropical oceans. They grow in shallow waters because they need sunlight to survive. They need warm water and waves that bring them food and oxygen.

The corals work together with tiny, microscopic plants called plant plankton that live inside it. Plant plankton converts sunlight into energy and feeds the coral. The coral also needs calcium to grow (calcium is a material in our bones and teeth). Corals are home to the most amazing sea creatures like sea urchins, sponges, sea stars, worms, fish, sharks, rays, lobster, shrimp, octopus, snails and many more. A quarter of all sea life lives among corals, although corals cover only 1% of the sea area.

Due to pollution, erosion, tourism and global warming, already 10% of the world's coral reefs have died. Scientists say that in the next 50 years many of the coral reefs on Earth will no longer exist. All the wonderful sea creatures that live among them will disappear. Humans need to stop polluting the seas and stop global warming to save the corals from dying.

Is it true? yes no

Corals grow deep down in the depths of the sea. ☐ ☐

Corals need cold water to live. ☐ ☐

Corals support a quarter of all sea life. ☐ ☐

Today, corals are healthy and growing in number. ☐ ☐

Humans are responsible for the corals dying. ☐ ☐

Humans can save the corals from dying. ☐ ☐

Read the text. Now read the sentences below and put a cross in the boxes according to whether they are true or false. This sheet may be photocopied by the purchaser. © Phonic Books Ltd 2016

Book 4: Comprehension quiz

Write the correct answer on the line.

1. The Coral Queen told Finn that deadly weeds had destroyed her _____.
a) sofa   b) kingdom   c) island   d) jewels

2. Finn dived into the sea with a bubble of air around his _____.
a) arm   b) hand   c) leg   d) head

3. The Coral Queen's palace was under_____.
a) sky   b) water   c) rocks   d) earth

4. Finn found the skyshard in an underwater _____.
a) chamber   b) street   c) tunnel   d) bricks

5. The black tendrils first grabbed his _____.
a) head   b) face   c) ankle   d) hair

6. The tendrils coiled so tightly around his body that Finn couldn't _____.
a) speak   b) sleep   c) dance   d) breathe

7. Finn managed to free himself with the help of _____.
a) Korus   b) the skyshard   c) the fish   d) the Coral Queen

8. When Finn surfaced, he held the skyshard _____.
a) aloft   b) on the ground   c) to his chest   d) in the waves

Book 4: Spelling assessment

1.

l	**ll**	**le**	**al**
like	all	little	final
lots	small	middle	medal
live	called	table	animal
let's	I'll	circle	mammal

2.

l	**ll**	**le**	**al**
love	full	simple	musical
self	spill	handle	signal
limp	he'll	temple	central
length	she'll	needle	crystal

This list can be used as a spelling assessment at the end of each unit of work. The teacher can add words from list 2 for able students. When dictating a word, say the word. Then say a sentence with the word in it (to put the word in the context of a sentence) and then repeat the word. E.g. "Rescue. I had to rescue the dog from the pond. Rescue." This ensures that the student has heard the word correctly. This sheet may be photocopied by the purchaser.

Book 4 – Line-up game 'l'

This game is for two players. Each player needs a batch of counters of one color. The players take turns to throw the die. They read a word in the column that corresponds to the number on the die and place their counter on that word. The first to have three of his/her counters in a row is the winner.

	leg	gobble	medal	plastic	simple	full
	null	total	miracle	troll	signal	table
	riddle	noble	last	handle	helpful	brilliant
	final	crystal	spell	belong	animal	critical
	trifle	refill	musical	central	coral	peddle

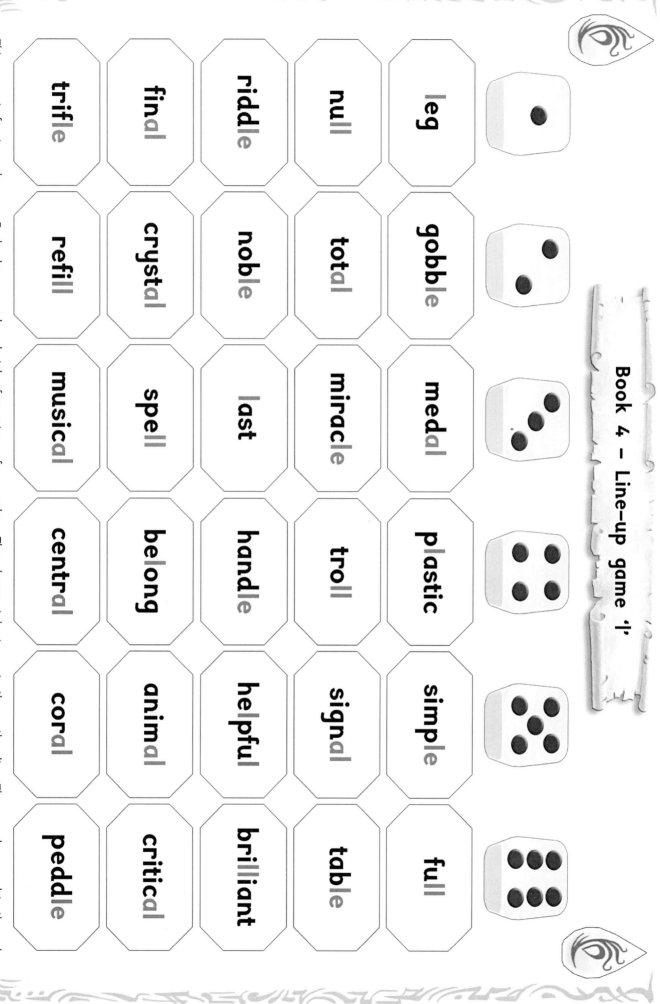

80

Book 5:   Blending and segmenting: 'j'

word						
just	j	u	s	t		
gem						
magic						
hinge						
giant						
range						
margin						
strange						
orange						
gentle						
danger						
plunge						
digest						

Blend the sounds and read the word. Segment the word into sounds by writing one sound in each square. This sheet may be photocopied by the purchaser. © Phonic Books Ltd 2016

Book 5: Reading and dictation 'j'

j

jump	☐
jungle	☐
jingle	☐
jumper	☐
jolly	☐

i

— — — —	☐
— — — — —	☐
— — — — —	☐
— — — — —	☐
— — — — —	☐

g

gem	☐
giant	☐
germ	☐
magic	☐
gentle	☐

g

— — —	☐
— — — —	☐
— — —	☐
— — — —	☐
— — — — —	☐

ge

hinge	☐
strange	☐
orange	☐
plunge	☐
range	☐

ge

— — — — —	☐
— — — — — —	☐
— — — — —	☐
— — — — —	☐
— — — —	☐

Fold the page along the dotted line. Ask the student to read the words on the left-hand side of the page. She/he can put a check next to them as he/she reads them. Turn over the folded page and dictate the same words to the student. He/she then opens up the page and checks his/her spelling with words in the left-hand column. This page may be photocopied by the purchaser. © Phonic Books Ltd 2016

Book 5: Reading and sorting words with 'j' spellings

j	g	ge

jumble	gist	tinge	jumper
gentle	giraffe	plunge	joke
gem	range	hinge	jungle
magic	damage	package	jogging
imagine	strange	jest	margin
bandage	tragic	digit	manage
jingle	general	giant	singe
savage	jagged	rigid	apology

Photocopy this page onto card and cut out the words. Read and sort the cards out according to the 'j' headings at the top of the page. The student can highlight the spellings of 'j' to help him/her read the words. The student can also list these words under the correct columns on the next page. This sheet may be photocopied by the purchaser. © Phonic Books Ltd 2016

Book 5: Reading and spelling 'j'

j	g	ge
_____	_____	_____
_____	_____	_____
_____	_____	_____
_____	_____	_____
_____	_____	_____
_____	_____	_____
_____	_____	_____
_____	_____	_____
_____	_____	_____
_____	_____	_____
_____	_____	_____
_____	_____	_____
_____	_____	_____
_____	_____	_____

Write the words in the correct column according to the spelling of 'j'. This sheet may be photocopied by the purchaser. © Phonic Books Ltd 2016

Book 5: Reading, sorting and spelling 'j'

j	g	ge
_____	_____	_____
_____	_____	_____
_____	_____	_____
_____	_____	_____
_____	_____	_____
_____	_____	_____
_____	_____	_____
_____	_____	_____
_____	_____	_____
_____	_____	_____

jingle   plunge   giant   magic   bandage   jolly

jasmine   manage   strange   germ   gentle   joking

hinge   margin   package   jumper   general   joy

tragic   savage   orange   major   junk   digit

digital   apology   garbage   singe   gem   engage

Write the words in the correct column according to the spelling of 'j'. This sheet may be photocopied by the purchaser. © Phonic Books Ltd 2016

Book 5: Chunking into syllables: 'j'

joking _____ / _____

giant _____ / _____

gentle _____ / _____

damage _____ / _____

storage _____ / _____

margin _____ / _____

magic _____ / _____

package _____ / _____

strangely _____ / _____

danger _____ / _____

bandage _____ / _____

tragic _____ / _____

justice _____ / _____

rigid _____ / _____

digital _____ / _____ / _____

general _____ / _____ / _____

imagine _____ / _____ / _____

Chunk the words into syllables and write the syllables on the lines. These words can also be used for dictation. This sheet may be photocopied by the purchaser. © Phonic Books Ltd 2016

Book 5: Reading and sorting words with <g> spelling

gap	gem

grit	gym	gulp	gel
girl	gate	giant	urgent
ginger	grand	germ	gust
gentle	giraffe	logic	glass
glue	biology	rigid	glance
flag	tragic	gabble	legend

Photocopy this page onto card and cut out the words. Read and sort the cards out according to sounds of the spelling <g>. The two sounds are: 'g' and 'j'. This sheet can also be used as a timed reading activity. This sheet may be photocopied by the purchaser.

Book 5: Questions for discussion

a) How many skyshards has Finn collected? (pages 1, 2)

b) What was 'unnatural' about the sea? (page 3)

c) Who was making the sea boil? (page 5)

d) Why do you think the Sea Spirit made the sea boil? (page 5)

e) Why did Finn feel exhausted? (page 7)

f) How did Finn and Korus fight the Sea Spirit? (pages 10, 11)

g) Why did Finn feel as if 'eels were wriggling in his veins'?

(page 13)

h) What happened to the Sea Spirit? (page 14)

i) What happened to Korus's feathers? (page 15)

j) What does 'Finn's energy was restored' mean? (page 16)

Book 5: What's missing in the picture?

Finn felt a shadow fall over him. He gazed upwards to see the massive head of a giant Sea Spirit. It had terrible, savage eyes. He saw the skyshard held in the huge watery head.

"Can we manage to get it?" he yelled. He jumped up to try and reach the skyshard, but then he felt all his energy drain away. He stumbled back, suddenly exhausted.

This is a comprehension activity. Read the text carefully and draw the missing details in the picture. This sheet may be photocopied by the purchaser. © Phonic Books Ltd 2016

Book 5: Reading fluency

The Sea Spirit was casting a spell. Finn felt his head droop. He slumped to the ground, barely able to keep himself awake.

"Sleep, sleep…" urged the giant Sea Spirit in a soft hiss. It began to inch dangerously close towards Finn and Korus. Finn shuddered as the vast watery body closed in on him. Korus lay slumped on the ground beside him, on the verge of sleep. Panic jolted Finn back to reality.

Suddenly, an idea sparked in Finn's head.

"A storm!" he yelled. "Wake up, Korus! We need to make a storm to release the energy in the skyshard!"

1st reading
_____ mins

2nd reading
_____ mins

3rd reading
_____ mins

Finn managed to shake Korus awake. Korus raised his beak and began to sing. All around, the sea began to churn. Clouds swirled in the darkening sky. As they merged and parted, cold drops of rain fell on Finn's face and helped him fight off sleep. He mustered all his energy and held the gauntlets up to the sky.

A massive storm blew up, thunder crashing from the blackened sky. The giant Sea Spirit gathered strength. He emerged from the sea in a towering cascade. He was poised for the final attack.

"Fly higher! You are in terrible danger!" cried Finn to Korus.

1st reading
_____ mins

2nd reading
_____ mins

3rd reading
_____ mins

This worksheet develops reading fluency. Each text box has approximately 100 words, based on the story in the series. Fold the sheet on the dotted line. Ask the student to read the first passage three times. Each attempt is timed. In the following lesson, the teacher can ask the student to read the next passage or both passages to increase reading stamina. This sheet can be photocopied by the purchaser.

Book 5: Punctuation

Capital letters, periods and question marks

Periods are needed at the end of sentences.

Question marks are needed at the end of sentences that are questions.

Capital letters are needed at the beginning of sentences and for proper nouns like names.

finn gazed at the symbol on the last skyshard
he shuddered it was a huge wave
where was the next skyshard
could it be in a wave he looked at it closely
that was not very logical

There are **7** capital letters, **5** periods and **2** question marks missing. Did you spot them all?

This is a punctuation and comprehension activity. Read the text carefully and find the missing periods, capital letters and question marks. This sheet may be photocopied by the purchaser.
© Phonic Books Ltd 2016

Book 5: Writing activity

Dear Mom,

So many things have happened since I last wrote! Today, we said farewell to the Coral Queen. Suddenly, the seas around Titan began to bubble. You just won't believe what happened next!

_____

_____

_____

_____

_____

_____

_____

_____

_____

Love Finn

Ask the student to retell the story using the pictures in the book. The teacher can list the order of events to help with the sequence of the story and/or provide vocabulary to help with writing fluency. The teacher can explain the genre of letter writing, its purpose and the kind of language used in this genre. This letter is a personal letter so the language should be informal, chatty and personal. The writer can engage the audience with humor and exaggeration. This sheet may be photocopied by the purchaser. © Phonic Books Ltd 2016

Book 5: New vocabulary – cloze activity

1. **cascade** – waterfall
2. **savage** – fierce
3. **barely** – hardly
4. **mustered** – gathered
5. **coax** – persuade
6. **poised** – wavering, on the brink of
7. **bid farewell** – say goodbye

Finn and Korus had to _____ to the Coral Queen. Finn was eager to get on, but Korus tried to _____ him to stay and eat some fish. Suddenly, the sea began to boil. Korus knew this was the work of a Sea Spirit. Just then, a huge and _____ Sea Spirit reared up from the sea. "The skyshard is MINE!" he hissed. Then he cast a spell. Finn felt his energy drain away. He could _____ keep awake. Panic jolted Finn back to reality. Suddenly, he had an idea.

"A storm!" Korus sang to the sea and started a storm.

Finn _____ all his energy and held the gauntlets up to the sky. The Sea Spirit emerged from the sea in a towering _____. He was _____ for the final attack.

Read and discuss new words with the student. Offer an example sentence with the new words if needed. The student can then give an example sentence. Ask the student to read the text and fill in the missing words and then reread the passage with the new vocabulary inserted in the text. This sheet may be photocopied by the purchaser. © Phonic Books Ltd 2016

Book 5: Comprehension – True or false?

Gauntlets

Gauntlets are gloves that cover the hands and the forearms (the arm above the wrist). They were part of a soldier's or knight's armor. They were very important because they protected the hands during hand–to–hand combat. Gauntlets were made of leather, chain mail, fabric or metal armor.

When soldiers started to use guns, they no longer fought hand–to–hand combat so gauntlets were not needed anymore. Today, gauntlets are used in sports like fencing and falconry (hunting with birds of prey). Some people use gauntlets to protect their hands if they have a dangerous job.

To 'throw down the gauntlet' is an old expression. It means to challenge someone to a fight. In the olden days, a knight would throw down his gauntlet if he wanted to challenge another knight to a duel. If the other knight wanted to fight, he would pick up the gauntlet and this would show that he accepted the challenge.

Is it true?	yes	no
Gauntlets protected the legs in battle.	☐	☐
Gauntlets were part of a knight's armor.	☐	☐
All gauntlets were made of metal.	☐	☐
Gauntlets are still used by soldiers today.	☐	☐
A knight threw down his gauntlet when he was sad.	☐	☐
To 'throw down the gauntlet' means to challenge someone.	☐	☐

Book 5: Comprehension quiz

Write the correct answer on the line.

1. Finn bid the Coral Queen _____.
a) hello   b) good day   c) farewell   d) good night

2. To 'coax' means to _____.
a) put on a coat   b) choke   c) yell   d) persuade

3. The Sea Spirit made the sea _____.
a) dazzle   b) boil   c) fry   d) shimmer

4. Finn felt his energy _____.
a) drain away   b) grow   c) pump   d) jump

5. Korus called the sea to make a _____.
a) noise   b) whirlpool   c) splash   d) storm

6. Lightning struck and _____ ran through the gauntlets.
a) oil   b) electricity   c) sun   d) water

7. The Sea Spirit _____ into the sea water.
a) dissolved   b) shrank   c) whisked   d) plunged

8. Korus's feathers were _____.
a) cooked   b) torn   c) shredded   d) singed

Book 5: Spelling assessment

1.

j	**g**	**ge**
June	magic	large
July	giant	change
just	ginger	strange
jump	giraffe	orange

- -

2.

j	**g**	**ge**
object	gentle	range
jumble	margin	lunge
jungle	germ	college
jacket	gigantic	village

This list can be used as a spelling assessment at the end of each unit of work. The teacher can add words from list 2 for able students. When dictating a word, say the word. Then say a sentence with the word in it (to put the word in the context of a sentence) and then repeat the word. E.g. "Rescue. I had to rescue the dog from the pond. Rescue." This ensures that the student has heard the word correctly. This sheet may be photocopied by the purchaser.

Book 5 – Line-up game 'j'

⚀	⚁	⚂	⚃	⚄	⚅
jam	germ	hinge	joke	strange	enjoy
general	object	merge	vegetable	jade	seige
college	gem	just	orange	ginger	rigid
margin	major	gentle	jump	garage	jelly
lunge	giant	reject	change	jacket	bulge

This game is for two players. Each player needs a batch of counters of one color. The players take turns to throw the die. They read a word in the column that corresponds to the number on the die and place their counter on that word. The first to have three of his/her counters in a row is the winner.

TITAN'S GAUNTLETS

Book 6
Phantoms of the Fog

Phoneme: 'f'
Spellings: f, ff, ph

Book 6: Blending and segmenting: 'f'

word							
flip	f	l	i	p			
huff							
phase							
photo							
fling							
staff							
orphan							
graph							
prophet							
dolphin							
phobia							
fluff							
alphabet							

Blend the sounds and read the word. Segment the word into sounds by writing one sound in each square. This sheet may be photocopied by the purchaser. © Phonic Books Ltd 2016

Book 6: Reading and dictation 'f'

f

felt	☐
flip	☐
food	☐
fight	☐
French	☐

f

☐ — — — —
☐ — — —
☐ — — —
☐ — — — —
☐ — — — — —

ff

puff	☐
stiff	☐
gruff	☐
staff	☐
off	☐

ff

☐ — — —
☐ — — — —
☐ — — — —
☐ — — —
☐ — —

ph

photo	☐
trophy	☐
dolphin	☐
orphan	☐
prophet	☐

ph

☐ — — — —
☐ — — — — —
☐ — — — — —
☐ — — — —
☐ — — — — —

Fold the page along the dotted line. Ask the student to read the words on the left-hand side of the page. She/he can put a check next to them as he/she reads them. Turn over the folded page and dictate the same words to the student. He/she then opens up the page and checks his/her spelling with words in the left-hand column. This page may be photocopied by the purchaser. © Phonic Books Ltd 2016

100

Book 6:   Reading and sorting words with 'f' spellings

f	ff	ph

photo	fist	stuff	trophy
elephant	gruff	physical	phantom
flint	flog	orphan	graph
prophet	fly	puffy	morph
alphabet	triumph	phoney	fright
flapping	decipher	phobia	toffee
frame	fresh	huffing	phonics
fret	coffee	flight	snuffle

Photocopy this page onto card and cut out the words. Read and sort the cards out according to the 'f' headings at the top of the page. The student can highlight the spellings of 'f' to help him/her read the words. The student can also list these words under the correct columns on the next page. This sheet may be photocopied by the purchaser. © Phonic Books Ltd 2016

Book 6: Reading and spelling 'f'

f	ff	ph
———	———	———
———	———	———
———	———	———
———	———	———
———	———	———
———	———	———
———	———	———
———	———	———
———	———	———
———	———	———
———	———	———
———	———	———
———	———	———
———	———	———

Book 6: Reading, sorting and spelling 'f'

f	ff	ph
_____	_____	_____
_____	_____	_____
_____	_____	_____
_____	_____	_____
_____	_____	_____
_____	_____	_____
_____	_____	_____
_____	_____	_____
_____	_____	_____
_____	_____	_____
_____	_____	_____

photo flint graph buffalo orphan flight fleck

phantom stiffly phase sniff flag trophy effect

prophet graphic truffle fence triumph coffee

funding dolphin physical bluff toffee friend

decipher phoney daffodil fresh

Write the words in the correct column according to the spelling of 'f'. This sheet may be photocopied by the purchaser. © Phonic Books Ltd 2016

Book 6: Chunking into syllables: 'f'

dolphin   _____ / _____

effort   _____ / _____

orphan   _____ / _____

firstly   _____ / _____

trophy   _____ / _____

bluffing   _____ / _____

prophet   _____ / _____

faulty   _____ / _____

giraffe   _____ / _____

graphic   _____ / _____

phoney   _____ / _____

typhoon   _____ / _____

different   _____ / _____ / _____

graffiti   _____ / _____ / _____

phobia   _____ / _____ / _____

alphabet   _____ / _____ / _____

elephant   _____ / _____ / _____

Book 6: Questions for discussion

a) How did Finn know he was going to meet pirates? (page 1)

b) 'Dolphins followed in their wake.' What does that mean? (page 2)

c) Why was the town 'battle-torn'? (page 3)

d) Why was there a 'whiff of sulphur' in the air? (page 3)

e) Why is Captain Tor called 'Salty'? (page 5)

f) Who had attacked the town? (page 5)

g) Salty did not think much of Finn and Korus. What changed his mind? (page 7)

h) What does the word 'cacophony' mean? (page 10)

i) Why did they have to sink Salty's ship? (page 14)

j) How did Salty help the town in the end? (page 16)

Book 6: What's missing in the picture?

Another phantom leaped forward and brandished his blade. Finn caught it with his gauntlet. He was struggling to keep the blade away from his face.

Suddenly, Salty was beside him. The phantom pirate slashed out at Salty.

"Salty, you have been hurt!" yelled Finn. "We must retreat!"

This is a comprehension activity. Read the text carefully and draw the missing details in the picture. This sheet may be photocopied by the purchaser. © Phonic Books Ltd 2016

Book 6: Reading fluency

"I am Captain Tor," his gruff voice rumbled. "People call me 'Salty' on account of my beard. This man is the mayor of the town."
"We have been attacked by phantom pirates," chipped in the mayor, "with catastrophic effect! I think they were looking for this!" He showed Finn and Korus a wooden box studded with sapphires. Inside it was the skyshard.
"They hijacked MY ship and MY cannons!" snapped Salty. "I think they're going to attack the town again!"
"We can help you in exchange for that jewel!" exclaimed Finn. Salty sucked on a salt crystal from his beard.

1st reading
_____ mins

2nd reading
_____ mins

3rd reading
_____ mins

How could this scruffy boy and his feeble bird beat a ship full of phantom pirates?
"Trust us, Salty!" said Korus.
Salty jumped. A talking bird! There was more to this pair than met the eye!
"Maybe they can help to save my treasure..." he thought.
Just before sunrise, the three of them set sail on a makeshift raft. Soon, the sails of Salty's ship came into view in the morning fog.
"Keep my ship safe!" Salty hissed emphatically. "That ship means more than family to me!"
They clambered up the side of the ship using fishing nets as footholds.

1st reading
_____ mins

2nd reading
_____ mins

3rd reading
_____ mins

This worksheet develops reading fluency. Each text box has approximately 100 words, based on the story in the series. Fold the sheet on the dotted line. Ask the student to read the first passage three times. Each attempt is timed. In the following lesson, the teacher can ask the student to read the next passage or both passages to increase reading stamina. This sheet can be photocopied by the purchaser.
© Phonic Books Ltd 2016

Book 6: Punctuation

Capital letters, periods and speech marks

Speech marks are used to show words that are spoken.

Remember to put any punctuation (like periods, commas and question marks) inside the speech marks.

Capital letters are needed at the beginning of sentences and for proper nouns like names.

Periods are needed at the end of sentences.

i am captain tor, a gruff voice rumbled

people call me 'salty' on account of my beard, he added

this town had been attacked by phantom pirates they hijacked my ship and my cannons to do it

There are **7** capital letters, **4** periods and **6** speech marks missing. Did you spot them all?

This is a punctuation and comprehension activity. Read the text carefully and find the missing periods, capital letters and speech marks. This sheet may be photocopied by the purchaser.
© Phonic Books Ltd 2016

Book 6: Writing activity

Character description – Salty

Why is Captain Tor called 'Salty'?

_____

_____

What is Salty like?

_____

_____

_____

_____

Do you think he is brave, loyal, greedy, selfish?
Why?_____

_____

_____

_____

Discuss the character of Salty in the book. Ask the student to give his/her opinion of Salty. An extension activity could be to write a story 'What Salty did next'. This sheet may be photocopied by the purchaser. © Phonic Books Ltd 2016

Book 6: New vocabulary – cloze activity

1. **phantom** – ghost
2. **waded** – walked through water
3. **sulphur** – an element used to make gun powder
4. **feeble** – weak
5. **makeshift** – temporary, not permanent
6. **billowing** – filling with air and swelling
7. **on account of** – because of

As Titan approached the island, they saw dark smoke

_____. Finn jumped into the water and _____ onto

the island. He could smell a whiff of _____.

Soon he met a sea captain.

"My name is Captain Tor," he said. "People call me 'Salty'

_____ my beard." The mayor told Finn and Korus that the

town had been attacked by _____ pirates.

Finn offered to help them. Salty didn't believe that such a scruffy

boy and a _____ bird could be of any help. That is, not

until Korus spoke. The next day, just before sunrise, they set sail

on a _____ raft.

Read and discuss new words with the student. Offer an example sentence with the new words if needed. The student can then give an example sentence. Ask the student to read the text and fill in the missing words and then reread the passage with the new vocabulary inserted in the text. This sheet may be photocopied by the purchaser. © Phonic Books Ltd 2016

Book 6: Comprehension – True or false?

Blackbeard, the pirate

Edward 'Blackbeard' Teach was one of the most feared and hated pirates of all time. He is thought to have lived in England before he became a pirate. He was named 'Blackbeard', because of his large, black beard that almost covered his entire face. To strike terror in the hearts of his enemies, Blackbeard would weave hemp (a plant used to make rope) into his hair, and light it so it looked like he was smoking from his head.

Edward Teach was a very large man. He carried two swords, many knives, and pistols. He was so scary that he was feared by his own crew. When he attacked other ships, if the crew surrendered, he would take their valuables and sail away. If they fought back, he would kill or maroon them (leave them on an island to die of hunger and thirst).

At the height of his success, Blackbeard commanded four pirate ships with 300 pirates on board. He had captured 40 ships and killed many people. In 1718, after five years of piracy, Blackbeard was killed in a battle with the Royal Navy. Although his career lasted only a few years, his reputation has long outlived him.

Is it true?

	yes	no
Blackbeard's real name was Edward Teach.	☐	☐
He was called 'Blackbeard' because of his long hair.	☐	☐
Many people were scared of Blackbeard.	☐	☐
Blackbeard captured 40 ships.	☐	☐
Blackbeard was a pirate for five years.	☐	☐
Blackbeard remained famous, even after his death.	☐	☐

Read the text. Now read the sentences below and put a cross in the boxes according to whether they are true or false. This sheet may be photocopied by the purchaser. © Phonic Books Ltd 2016

Book 6: Comprehension quiz

Write the correct answer on the line.

1. The skull and bones symbol on the shard represented _____.
a) princes   b) pirates   c) people   d) monsters

2. The pirates had attacked the town with _____.
a) guns   b) axes   c) rifles   d) cannons

3. Captain Tor was called 'Salty' on account of his _____.
a) hair   b) coat   c) hat   d) beard

4. The shard was in a _____–studded box.
a) sapphire   b) ruby   c) diamond   d) gold

5. Finn and Salty fought the phantom _____.
a) birds   b) pirates   c) soldiers   d) tigers

6. The word 'cacophony' means terrible _____.
a) humming   b) drumming   c) scratching   d) noise

7. Salty was sad to see his beloved ship _____.
a) sink   b) drift   c) float   d) tilt

8. Korus suggested that Salty give the mayor some _____.
a) silver coins   b) copper coins   c) gold coins   d) brass coins

jBook 6: Spelling assessment

1.

f	**ff**	**ph**
fast	stuff	phone
find	offer	photo
before	suffer	graph
friends	different	elephant

2,

f	**ff**	**ph**
after	effort	orphan
first	afford	sphere
fright	coffee	phantom
fair	offend	alphabet

This list can be used as a spelling assessment at the end of each unit of work. The teacher can add words from list 2 for able students. When dictating a word, say the word. Then say a sentence with the word in it (to put the word in the context of a sentence) and then repeat the word. E.g. "Rescue. I had to rescue the dog from the pond. Rescue." This ensures that the student has heard the word correctly. This sheet may be photocopied by the purchaser.

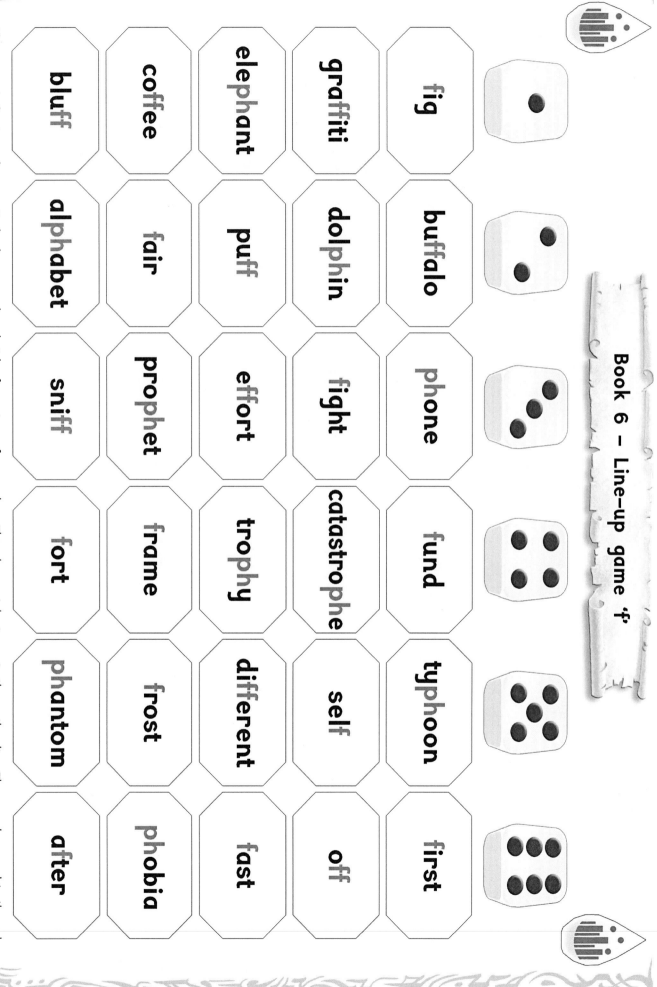

Book 6 – Line-up game 'f'

This game is for two players. Each player needs a batch of counters of one color. The players take turns to throw the die. They read a word in the column that corresponds to the number on the die and place their counter on that word. The first to have three of his/her counters in a row is the winner.

(1)	(2)	(3)	(4)	(5)	(6)
fig	buffalo	phone	fund	typhoon	first
graffiti	dolphin	fight	catastrophe	self	off
elephant	puff	effort	trophy	different	fast
coffee	fair	prophet	frame	frost	phobia
bluff	alphabet	sniff	fort	phantom	after

TITAN'S GAUNTLETS

Book 7
Unnatural Creatures

Suffix: <-ture>

Book 7: Blending and segmenting: <ture>

capture	c	a	p	ture
culture				
mixture				
future				
vulture				
torture				
creature				
nature				
adventure						
departure					
texture				
structure						
signature						

Blend the sounds and read the word. Segment the word into sounds by writing one sound in each square. This sheet may be photocopied by the purchaser. © Phonic Books Ltd 2016

Book 7: Reading and dictation <ture>

ture

nature	☐
capture	☐
future	☐
vulture	☐
mixture	☐
adventure	☐
puncture	☐
signature	☐
departure	☐
creature	☐
feature	☐
fracture	☐
torture	☐
vulture	☐
scripture	☐

ture

Fold the page along the dotted line. Ask the student to read the words on the left-hand side of the page. She/he can put a check next to them as he/she reads them. Turn over the folded page and dictate the same words to the student. He/she then opens up the page and checks his/her spelling with words in the left-hand column. This page may be photocopied by the purchaser. © Phonic Books Ltd 2016

Book 7: Reading practice – words with <ture> (highlighted)

pasture	culture	creature	mixture
caricature	miniature	lecture	posture
nature	gesture	puncture	picture
torture	future	fixture	feature
texture	vulture	structure	signature
capture	scripture	departure	fracture

Use this page to practice reading words with the suffix <ture>. This sheet may be photocopied by the purchaser. © Phonic Books Ltd 2016

Book 7: Reading practice – words with <ture>

pasture	culture	creature	mixture
caricature	miniature	lecture	posture
nature	gesture	puncture	picture
torture	future	fixture	feature
texture	vulture	structure	signature
capture	scripture	departure	fracture

Use this page to practice reading words with the suffix <ture>. The student can highlight the suffix to help him/her read the words. This sheet may be photocopied by the purchaser. © Phonic Books Ltd 2016

Book 7: Reading and spelling <ture>

ture

_____

_____

_____

_____

_____

_____

_____

_____

_____

_____

_____

_____

_____

_____

_____

Reread Book 7 and find the words with the <ture> suffix. List these words in the column above.
This sheet may be photocopied by the purchaser. © Phonic Books Ltd 2016

Book 7: Chunking into syllables: <ture>

picture _____/_____

mixture _____/_____

capture _____/_____

gesture _____/_____

future _____/_____

creature _____/_____

feature _____/_____

nature _____/_____

pasture _____/_____

puncture _____/_____

fixture _____/_____

torture _____/_____

departure _____/_____/_____

signature _____/_____/_____

adventure _____/_____/_____

caricature _____/_____/_____/_____

temperature _____/_____/_____/_____

Chunk the words into syllables and write the syllables on the lines. These words can also be used for dictation. This sheet may be photocopied by the purchaser. © Phonic Books Ltd 2016

122

Book 7: Questions for discussion

a) The new shard had three circles above some pipes. What did that symbolize? (page 2)

b) Titan seemed to stand higher in the water. Why? (page 4)

c) 'A light shimmered from an archway'. What does 'shimmer' mean? (page 5)

d) What did Salty, Finn and Korus find inside the cavern? (page 6)

e) What are sentinels? (page 7)

f) What were the sentinels guarding? (page 9)

g) Why did the statues start to move? (page 10)

h) Where was the skyshard hidden? (page 12)

i) What happened to the sentinels? (page 14)

j) How did Salty help to release Korus from the sentinel's stone hand? (page 15)

Book 7: What's missing in the picture?

Salty traced the textured marks on the structure with his fingers. "These markings are not from any culture I know," he said.

"The statues give me the creeps," Finn said with a shudder. The posture made them seem like guards.

"Yes, they look like sentinels," said Salty.

This is a comprehension activity. Read the text carefully and draw the missing details in the picture. This sheet may be photocopied by the purchaser. © Phonic Books Ltd 2016

124

Book 7: Reading fluency

Korus stared at the strange words scratched into the stone.

"I think it's some kind of organ!" said Finn. He blew into one of the pipes and a round marble ball emerged. The ball rose and fell as he blew. It was magical! He was starting to enjoy his adventure on this island after all.

"I have translated these strange symbols," said Korus. "A skyshard is hidden here. We can only find it if we play the right tune on the organ!" Salty and Korus began to blow.

"We need to copy the symbol on the skyshard!" Finn realized.

1st reading

_____ mins

2nd reading

_____ mins

3rd reading

_____ mins

- -

Salty struggled to blow gently. His marble was caught by the wind and crashed lifeless to the ground. At once, the rocks began to fracture.

"The statues are moving!" screamed Finn. The stone creatures broke free of the vines that nature had grown around them. They shuddered into life.

Korus shook with fear.

"These stone monsters are hovering all around us like vultures. They'll capture us or kill us!" he screeched.

"Run!" yelled Salty as he gestured at the stone walls. "The cavern is about to collapse!"

This gave Finn an idea. He crashed his fist into the stone wall.

1st reading

_____ mins

2nd reading

_____ mins

3rd reading

_____ mins

This worksheet develops reading fluency. Each text box has approximately 100 words, based on the story in the series. Fold the sheet on the dotted line. Ask the student to read the first passage three times. Each attempt is timed. In the following lesson, the teacher can ask the student to read the next passage or both passages to increase reading stamina. This sheet can be photocopied by the purchaser.
© Phonic Books Ltd 2016

Book 7: Punctuation

Exclamation marks, question marks and speech marks

Question marks are used at the end of questions.

Exclamation marks tell the reader to read with expression such as anger, excitement or surprise.

Speech marks are used to show words that are spoken.

Remember to put any punctuation (like periods, commas and question marks) inside the speech marks.

Do you think the skyshard really meant this island asked Finn.

The storm raged and Titan was hurled against the rocky cliffside.

If this storm carries on, Titan will fracture something shouted Salty

There are **4** speech marks, **1** question mark and **1** exclamation mark missing. Did you spot them all?

This is a punctuation and comprehension activity. Discuss with the student when the punctuation marks practiced above are used, and why. Ask the student to read the text carefully and find the missing speech marks, question marks and exclamation marks. An extension activity could be to ask the student to write his/her own passage using this punctuation. This sheet may be photocopied by the purchaser. © Phonic Books Ltd 2016

Book 7: Writing activity

Island News

CAPTAIN, BIRD AND BOY FIND SKYSHARD IN COLLAPSING CAVERN

By _____

Captain Tor (AKA 'Salty'), a boy and a talking bird emerged with a skyshard from a collapsing cavern. They came out dazed, but unharmed. Our reporter, _____, reports from the scene.

There was debris everywhere! As the dust settled, three figures emerged from the collapsed cavern. I grabbed hold of _____. This is what he told me:

"

_____

_____

_____

_____

_____

_____

_____

_____

_____

"

Ask the student to choose a character (Salty, Finn or Korus) and to imagine that he/she is a reporter interviewing him. Discuss how the chosen character would speak. This sheet may be photocopied by the purchaser. © Phonic Books Ltd 2016

Book 7: New vocabulary – cloze activity

1. **textured** – having a rough surface
2. **brewing** – forming (of a storm)
3. **fragments** – broken pieces
4. **cavern** – a large cave
5. **fracture** – break or crack
6. **gestured** – pointed
7. **stirring** – waking up, rousing

The crashing waves beat against Titan's side. A storm was

_____. Finn was nervous.

"I don't want to venture off Titan and onto to THAT!" He

_____ at the rocky cliffside of the island.   Titan was hurled

against the cliff. _____ dropped into the sea. Finn was

worried that part of Titan would _____. Titan seemed to

stand higher in the water than he had before. It was as though

he was slowly _____ as Finn collected the skyshards.

They leaped across onto a ledge and struggled up the cliff. They

discovered an amazing _____. Inside the cavern stood a

strange organ with _____ markings on it.

Book 7: Comprehension – True or false?

The Terra Cotta Army

In 1974, farmers in the Shaanxi province of China began to dig a well. They uncovered a massive army of 8,000 lifesize clay sculptures of Chinese soldiers. They were part of the grave of China's first Emperor, Qin Shi Huang. He died more than 2,000 years ago. Emperor Qin wanted this army to protect him in the afterlife – the life after his death.

What is so amazing is that all the soldiers look different. They wear different uniforms from different parts of the army and different ranks. They have different hair styles and different facial expressions. There were also hundreds of horses and even chariots in this huge grave. Archaeologists believe that about 700,000 workers worked for several years to create this army. They had moulds and they would work like a factory. One person made legs, another made heads, another made the bodies. The parts were then assembled together and personal features like hair and moustaches were added at the end. Terra cotta is a kind of clay. This is why it is called the Terra Cotta Army.

Is it true?	yes	no
Emperor Qin died in 1974.	☐	☐
The Emperor believed that he would live after his death.	☐	☐
The clay soldiers were made to protect the Emperor.	☐	☐
There were no clay animals in the grave.	☐	☐
All the clay soldiers looked the same.	☐	☐
Terra cotta is a kind of stone.	☐	☐

Read the text. Now read the sentences below and put a cross in the boxes according to whether they are true or false. This sheet may be photocopied by the purchaser. © Phonic Books Ltd 2016

Book 7: Comprehension quiz

Write the correct answer on the line.

1. The symbol on the shard represented the organ and _____.
a) footballs   b) marbles   c) peas   d) sweets

2. Titan was stirring because Finn had collected _____.
a) feathers   b) beads   c) gold   d) skyshards

3. A cavern is a large _____.
a) cave   b) hole   c) rock   d) stone

4. Salty and Finn blew on the _____ pipes.
a) flute   b) trumpet   c) organ   d) clarinet

5. 'The rocks began to fracture' means they began to _____.
a) slide   b) crack   c) grow   d) melt

6. The word 'sentinel' means _____.
a) soldier   b) man   c) fighter   d) guard

7. Salty uses a _____ to cut Korus from the grip of the sentinel.
a) stone   b) diamond   c) knife   d) axe

8. Salty stays behind on the _____.
a) pier   b) boat   c) island   d) mountain

Book 7: Spelling assessment

-ture

picture

mixture

adventure

creature

capture

structure

nature

furniture

This list can be used as a spelling assessment at the end of each unit of work. The teacher can add words from list 2 for able students. When dictating a word, say the word. Then say a sentence with the word in it (to put the word in the context of a sentence) and then repeat the word. E.g. "Rescue. I had to rescue the dog from the pond. Rescue." This ensures that the student has heard the word correctly. This sheet may be photocopied by the purchaser.

Book 7 – Line-up game <ture>

(1)	(2)	(3)	(4)	(5)	(6)
capture	adventure	culture	mixture	feature	creature
departure	caricature	future	nature	puncture	signature
fracture	fixture	gesture	mature	literature	moisture
nurture	pasture	recapture	scripture	sculpture	torture
venture	vulture	miniature	rupture	posture	immature

TITAN'S GAUNTLETS

Book 8
A Strange Location

Suffix: <-tion>

Book 8: Blending and segmenting: <tion>

station	s	t	a	tion
mention				
ration				
action				
option				
addition				
direction						
election					
reaction					
solution					
situation						
position					
lotion				

Book 8: Reading and dictation <tion>

tion

action	☐
mention	☐
position	☐
station	☐
potion	☐
fraction	☐
addition	☐
ignition	☐
ration	☐
nation	☐
option	☐
creation	☐
solution	☐
situation	☐
function	☐

tion

Fold the page along the dotted line. Ask the student to read the words on the left-hand side of the page. She/he can put a check next to them as he/she reads them. Turn over the folded page and dictate the same words to the student. He/she then opens up the page and checks his/her spelling with words in the left-hand column. This page may be photocopied by the purchaser. © Phonic Books Ltd 2016

Book 8: Reading practice – words with <tion> (highlighted)

relation	action	situation	education
solution	evolution	reaction	option
deduction	motion	position	mention
lotion	invitation	formation	nation
direction	sensation	hesitation	insulation
vegetation	irritation	revelation	caution
revolution	ignition	potion	caption

Use this page to practice reading words with the suffix <tion>. This sheet may be photocopied by the purchaser. © Phonic Books Ltd 2016

Book 8: Reading practice – words with <tion>

relation	action	situation	education
solution	evolution	reaction	option
deduction	motion	position	mention
lotion	invitation	formation	nation
direction	sensation	hesitation	insulation
vegetation	irritation	revelation	caution
revolution	ignition	potion	caption

Use this page to practice reading words with the suffix <tion>. The student can highlight the suffix to help him/her read the words. This sheet may be photocopied by the purchaser.
© Phonic Books Ltd 2016

Book 8: Reading and spelling <tion>

tion

_____

_____

_____

_____

_____

_____

_____

_____

_____

_____

_____

_____

_____

_____

_____

_____

Reread Book 8 and find the words with the suffix <tion>. List these words in the column above.

Book 8: Chunking into syllables: <tion>

action	_____ / _____
lotion	_____ / _____
mention	_____ / _____
nation	_____ / _____
station	_____ / _____
ration	_____ / _____
caution	_____ / _____
option	_____ / _____
position	_____ / _____ / _____
solution	_____ / _____ / _____
direction	_____ / _____ / _____
connection	_____ / _____ / _____
relation	_____ / _____ / _____
reaction	_____ / _____ / _____
calculation	_____ / _____ / _____ / _____
information	_____ / _____ / _____ / _____
situation	_____ / _____ / _____ / _____

Chunk the words into syllables and write the syllables on the lines. These words can also be used for dictation. This sheet may be photocopied by the purchaser. © Phonic Books Ltd 2016

Book 8: Questions for discussion

a) The new shard had a huge eye on it. What do you think that

   represented? (page 1)

b) Who lived in the strange caves up the side of the volcano? (page 2)

c) When they meet the furballs, Korus says: "A little more caution is

   my suggestion!" Why? (page 4)

d) The furballs felt desolation. What does that mean? (page 5)

e) Why were the furballs hungry? (pages 6 and 9)

f) Finn punched the air with elation when he got the skyshard. Why?

   (page 7)

g) What did the one–eyed mutant beast do to the oldest furball?

   (page 10)

h) How did Finn defeat the one–eyed mutant beast? (page 13)

i) Finn wanted to take the furball with him. Do you think that was a

   good idea? Explain. (page 15)

j) How do you think the furballs felt when the mutant was defeated?

   (page 16)

Book 8: What's missing in the picture?

"What a strange location..." muttered Finn. A thousand

eyes peered out of cave dwellings in the cliffs. With a

shuddering action, Titan pointed a rocky finger in the

direction of a path in the cliffs. It snaked up the side of

the volcano.

"Titan's giving us an instruction!" cried Finn in

astonishment.

142

Book 8: Reading fluency

A crowd of furry beings burst from the shadows and swarmed around them.

"These furballs have more hair than Salty!" joked Finn. Then he made a surprising observation. "They only have one eye!"

Korus looked at them with trepidation. "A little more caution – is my suggestion," he warned.
Finn sensed a terrible desolation coming from the furballs. They were gesturing towards their mouths and stomachs. Korus plucked a fish from the water. He was still wary of the furballs. "I might mention here that they seem very hungry," he noted. The furballs gazed at the fish hungrily.

1st reading

_____ mins

2nd reading

_____ mins

3rd reading

_____ mins

Finn had a sudden realization. "They are on the verge of starvation!" he cried. Korus looked at the island's dense vegetation and made a suggestion.
"We could teach them how to weave fishing nets from vines," he said.

The nets were a great solution. Many fish were caught. "A celebration meal!" chirped Korus happily. At the campfire, the oldest furball stepped forward. He presented Finn with a necklace. At the end of it hung the skyshard.

"The skyshard!" yelled Finn, punching the air with elation. Finn had a terrible sensation that he was being watched. Suddenly, they heard an evil cackle.

1st reading

_____ mins

2nd reading

_____ mins

3rd reading

_____ mins

This worksheet develops reading fluency. Each text box has approximately 100 words, based on the story in the series. Fold the sheet on the dotted line. Ask the student to read the first passage three times. Each attempt is timed. In the following lesson, the teacher can ask the student to read the next passage or both passages to increase reading stamina. This sheet can be photocopied by the purchaser.
© Phonic Books Ltd 2016

Book 8: Punctuation

Exclamation marks and speech marks

Speech marks are used to show words that are spoken.

Remember to put any punctuation (like periods, commas and question marks) inside the speech marks.

Exclamation marks tell the reader to read with expression such as anger, excitement or surprise.

The skyshard is MINE bellowed the mutant beast.

We must flee We have no other option screeched Korus.

Look The mutant beast is hypnotizing them said Finn.

There are **6** speech marks and **5** exclamation marks.   Did you spot them all?

This is a punctuation and comprehension activity. Read the text carefully and find the missing speech marks and exclamation marks. This sheet may be photocopied by the purchaser.

Book 8: Writing activity

Island News

Boy and Talking Bird Save Furballs on Volcano Island

By _____

Finn, a boy and Korus, a magical talking bird, discovered strange, captive furballs on Volcano Island. Finn managed to set them free after defeating the one-eyed mutant beast who kept them as slaves.

Our reporter, _____, reports from Volcano Island.

_____

_____

_____

_____

_____

_____

_____

_____

_____

_____

Ask the student to recount how Finn and Korus saved the furballs from the mutant beast. This sheet may be photocopied by the purchaser. © Phonic Books Ltd 2016

Book 8: New vocabulary – cloze activity

1. **determination** – decided on a purpose
2. **destination** – a place to which someone is traveling
3. **prediction** – a forecast, tell the future
4. **desolation** – a feeling of being abandoned and hopeless
5. **anticipation** – expecting something
6. **motion** – movement
7. **elation** – a feeling of great joy

With a rocking _____, Titan came to a stop at a volcanic island. Finn looked at the skyshard and made a _____. The next creature would be a wild beast! He gazed up towards the volcano. Was this their next _____? Finn leaped onto the island. He was full of excitement and _____. Suddenly, they were surrounded by furry beings. Korus was nervous. The furballs looked sad. Finn sensed a terrible _____ coming from them. Korus saw that they looked hungry. He taught them to make fishing nets. Then, the oldest furball presented Finn with the skyshard. "The skyshard!" he yelled and punched the air with _____. Suddenly, a one-eyed mutant beast burst out of the dark space. He hypnotized the furballs. They marched towards Finn with _____.

Book 8: Comprehension – True or false?

Volcanoes

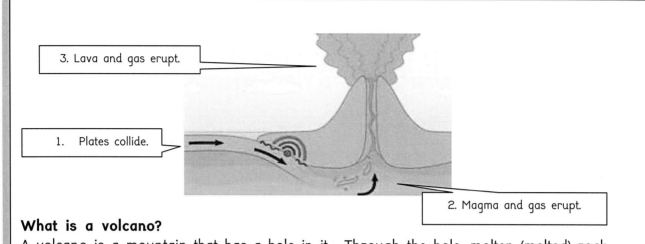

3. Lava and gas erupt.

1. Plates collide.

2. Magma and gas erupt.

What is a volcano?
A volcano is a mountain that has a hole in it. Through the hole, molten (melted) rock called magma and gas burst out. The magma and gas lie under the crust of the Earth. The word 'volcano' comes from the Roman God of Fire, Vulcan. There are 1,510 active volcanoes in the world. Some of them are under the sea.

Why do volcanoes erupt?
The Earth is made of three layers. The outer layer that we live on is called the 'crust'. Underneath it is the 'mantle'. Under the mantle is the 'core' – the center of the Earth. The Earth's crust is made of plates like giant jigsaw puzzles. When they collide, one may go over another. This causes the magma to erupt. It's like a pressure cooker that needs to blast out. The magma that erupts out onto the surface is called 'lava'. When lava flows down the volcano, it is extremely hot. It is red or white hot. As the lava flows, it cools and becomes thicker. It then turns into solid rock.

Is it true?	yes	no
Volcanoes are mountains that are always on land.	☐	☐
The word 'volcano' comes from the Roman God, Vulcan.	☐	☐
'Erupts' means bursts out.	☐	☐
Volcanoes erupt when the Earth's plates collide.	☐	☐
Magma is the boiling hot rock inside the volcano.	☐	☐
The lava cools and then it turns into rock.	☐	☐

Read the text. Now read the sentences below and put a cross in the boxes according to whether they are true or false. This sheet may be photocopied by the purchaser. © Phonic Books Ltd 2016

Book 8: Comprehension quiz

Write the correct answer on the line.

1. The creatures living inside the volcano mountain were _____.
a) footballs   b) furballs   c) basketballs   d) handballs

2. Titan pointed his finger at a _____ snaking up the volcano.
a) house   b) road   c) path   d) cloud

3. The furballs had only one _____.
a) eye   b) ear   c) hand   d) leg

4. The furballs were _____.
a) silly   b) happy   c) dizzy   d) hungry

5. 'Elation' means _____.
a) sleepiness   b) great hunger   c) great joy   d) foolishness

6. The one-eyed beast controlled the furballs by _____ them.
a) hitting   b) hypnotizing   c) fighting   d) eating

7. The mutant beast was buried under a pile of _____.
a) rocks   b) papers   c) apples   d) boxes

8. 'Plummets' means _____.
a) flies up   b) swims   c) dances   d) drops straight down

Book 8: Spelling assessment

–tion

nation

station

information

addition

subtraction

competition

invention

education

This list can be used as a spelling assessment at the end of each unit of work. The teacher can add words from list 2 for able students. When dictating a word, say the word. Then say a sentence with the word in it (to put the word in the context of a sentence) and then repeat the word. E.g. "Rescue. I had to rescue the dog from the pond. Rescue." This ensures that the student has heard the word correctly. This sheet may be photocopied by the purchaser.
© Phonic Books Ltd 2016

Book 8 – Line-up game <tion>

This game is for two players. Each player needs a batch of counters of one color. The players take turns to throw the die. They read a word in the column that corresponds to the number on the die and place their counter on that word. The first to have three of his/her counters in a row is the winner.

•	••	•••	••••	•••••	••••••
action	motion	fraction	addition	caption	caution
creation	direction	formation	function	elation	invitation
jubilation	hesitation	fiction	dictionary	inspection	potion
dictation	collection	condition	connection	description	education
nation	stationary	relation	option	position	reflection

TITAN'S GAUNTLETS

Book 9
Artificial Heart

Suffixes: <-tial> and <-cial>

152

Book 9: Blending and segmenting: <cial>, <tial>

facial | f | a | cial

special

martial

official

potential

financial

torrential

artificial

essential

racial

social

beneficial

glacial

Blend the sounds and read the word. Segment the word into sounds by writing one sound in each square. This sheet may be photocopied by the purchaser. © Phonic Books Ltd 2016

Book 9: Reading and dictation <cial> <tial>

cial

social	☐
special	☐
racial	☐
glacial	☐
official	☐

cial

___ __ _____	☐
___ ___ _____	☐
___ __ _____	☐
___ ___ _____	☐
___ ___ __ _____	☐

tial

initial	☐
potential	☐
martial	☐
spatial	☐
essential	☐

tial

___ ___ _____	☐
___ ___ __ ____	☐
___ ___ _____	☐
___ ___ _____	☐
___ ___ ___ __	☐

Fold the page along the dotted line. Ask the student to read the words on the left-hand side of the page. She/he can put a check next to them as he/she reads them. Turn over the folded page and dictate the same words to the student. He/she then opens up the page and checks his/her spelling with words in the left-hand column. This page may be photocopied by the purchaser. © Phonic Books Ltd 2016

Book 9: Reading words with <cial> and <tial> (highlighted)

cial	tial

official 1	glacial 2	essential 3	partial 4
racial 5	initial 6	influential 7	social 8
torrential 9	commercial 10	facial 11	confidential 12

having influence on something or somebody 7	coming from an authority e.g. 'an official letter' 1	like a fast stream of water e.g. 'torrential rain' 9	relating to only a part of something 4
the beginning of something 6	absolutely necessary 3	relating to dividing humans according to their race 5	relating to living in a community 8
to do with the face e.g. beauty treatment to face 11	to do with buying and selling for profit 10	icy 2	spoken or given in private 12

Photocopy this page onto card and cut out the words and the definitions. Match the definitions to the words, using the numbers and stick them back to back. Read the cards with the suffixes and sort them into the two different spellings. This sheet may be photocopied by the purchaser. © Phonic Books Ltd 2016

Book 9: Reading words with <cial> and <tial>

cial	tial

official	glacial	essential	partial
racial	initial	influential	social
torrential	commercial	facial	confidential

relating to only a part of something	relating to living in a community	having influence on something or somebody	relating to dividing humans according to their race
like a fast stream of water e.g. 'torrential rain'	to do with buying and selling for profit	to do with the face e.g. beauty treatment to face	coming from an authority e.g. 'an official letter'
icy	the beginning of something	spoken or given in private	absolutely necessary

Photocopy this page onto card and cut out the words and the definitions. Match the definitions to the words and stick them back to back. Read the words and sort according to the two different spellings. This sheet may be photocopied by the purchaser. © Phonic Books Ltd 2016

Book 9: Reading and spelling <cial> and <tial>

cial	tial
_____	_____
_____	_____
_____	_____
_____	_____
_____	_____
_____	_____
_____	_____
_____	_____
_____	_____
_____	_____

Reread Book 9 and find the words with the suffixes <cial> and <tial>. List these words in the columns above. This sheet may be photocopied by the purchaser. © Phonic Books Ltd 2016

Book 9: Chunking into syllables: <cial> <tial>

social   _____/_____

spacial   _____/_____

partial   _____/_____

special   _____/_____

crucial   _____/_____

martial   _____/_____

facial   _____/_____

potential   _____/_____/_____

financial   _____/_____/_____

torrential   _____/_____/_____

substantial   _____/_____/_____

commercial   _____/_____/_____

official   _____/_____/_____

essential   _____/_____/_____

beneficial   _____/_____/_____/_____

residential   _____/_____/_____/_____

confidential   _____/_____/_____/_____

Book 9: Questions for discussion

a) Finn knew it was crucial to understand the symbols on the skyshards. Why? (page 2)

b) Why were the people desperately waving at Finn? (page 4)

c) A substantial part of Titan's body was now above sea level. What does that mean? (page 6)

d) Who do you think was controlling the flying machines? (page 7)

e) Who had imprisoned the people in the fortress? (page 8)

f) How did Finn get into the fortress? (page 9)

g) How did Finn get the salt water to knock over the metal soldiers? (page 11)

h) From above, Finn and Korus looked down at the spacial layout of the fortress. What does that mean? (page 12)

i) Where was the skyshard hidden? (page 13)

j) What happened to the evil inventor in the end? (page 15)

Book 9: What's missing in the picture?

A substantial part of Titan's body was now above sea level. Finn took cover under his rocky forearms as the attackers bombarded them.

"Do something, Korus!" yelled Finn. "Use your influential power with the sea NOW!"

Korus opened his beak and sang his magic to the sea.

This is a comprehension activity. Read the text carefully and draw the missing details in the picture. This sheet may be photocopied by the purchaser. © Phonic Books Ltd 2016

Book 9: Reading fluency

The latest skyshard was especially sharp. It cut Finn's finger. Luckily, the wound was superficial.
"The symbol looks like a heart within a kind of cog," he told Korus nervously. His recent experience with the one-eyed monster had taught him one thing: it was crucial to understand the symbols on the skyshard.

Titan headed into a mist. "I can't see where we are heading!" yelled Finn. The mist partially blocked his view. Then, as if from nowhere, an iron fortress loomed before them. It was huge! The top was shrouded in clouds. From afar, Finn could see people waving at them.

| 1st reading |
| _____ mins |

| 2nd reading |
| _____ mins |

| 3rd reading |
| _____ mins |

"Look at the base of the tower!" squawked Korus.
"There are people trapped in there!"
"We have to help!" yelled Finn.

At last, the storm began to die. Titan approached the fortress. Finn looked up. He could see dark shadows in the clouds above him.
"Finn, it is essential that you take cover RIGHT NOW!" warned Korus. Strange flying machines were heading straight at him.

A substantial part of Titan's body was now above sea level. Finn took cover under his rocky forearm as the attackers bombarded them. "Do something, Korus! Use your influential power with the sea!" yelled Finn.

| 1st reading |
| _____ mins |

| 2nd reading |
| _____ mins |

| 3rd reading |
| _____ mins |

This worksheet develops reading fluency. Each text box has approximately 100 words, based on the story in the series. Fold the sheet on the dotted line. Ask the student to read the first passage three times. Each attempt is timed. In the following lesson, the teacher can ask the student to read the next passage or both passages to increase reading stamina. This sheet can be photocopied by the purchaser.
© Phonic Books Ltd 2016

Book 9: Punctuation

Capital letters, periods, question marks and speech marks

Speech marks are used to show words that are spoken.

Remember to put any punctuation (like periods, commas and question marks) inside the speech marks.

how can I get in the fortress asked finn there is a special entrance underwater, said the owner's wife

finn dived into the sea he was gripped by fear would he make it into the tunnel

There are **6** capital letters, **4** speech marks, **2** question marks and **4** periods missing. Did you spot them all?

This is a punctuation and comprehension activity. Read the text carefully and find the missing capital letters, speech marks, question marks and periods. This sheet may be photocopied by the purchaser. © Phonic Books Ltd 2016

Book 9: Writing activity

Write a short blurb for the back cover of the series.

Ask the student to read the blurb on the back of the Titan's Gauntlets series. Discuss the purpose of a back cover blurb. How much information should be offered about characters and plot? How does the blurb entice the reader to start reading the series? Ask the student to write his/her own blurb for the series. This sheet may be photocopied by the purchaser. © Phonic Books Ltd 2016

Book 9: New vocabulary – cloze activity

1. **superficial** – existing on the surface
2. **partially** – only in part
3. **facial expressions** – the looks on their faces
4. **substantial** – a large amount
5. **influential** – having influence on someone
6. **torrential** – heavy rain falling
7. **artificial** – unnatural

The latest skyshard was very sharp. It cut Finn's finger. Luckily, the wound was only _____. Another _____ storm was brewing up. There was a mist ahead. Suddenly, a fortress loomed from the mist. It was _____ hidden in the clouds. At the base of the tower, Finn could see people waving frantically. He couldn't see their _____. The storm died down. Finn noticed that a _____ part of Titan's body was now above sea level. Then they were attacked by flying machines. "Korus! Do something! Use your _____ power with the sea NOW!" cried Finn. Korus sang to the sea. A huge spiral of water rose and smashed the flying machines. There was something strangely _____ about them.

Read and discuss new words with the student. Offer an example sentence with the new words if needed. The student can then give an example sentence. Ask the student to read the text and fill in the missing words and then reread the passage with the new vocabulary inserted in the text. This sheet may be photocopied by the purchaser. © Phonic Books Ltd 2016

Book 9: Comprehension – True or false?

Facts about flying and flying machines

The first flying machine was invented by the Wright brothers in 1903.

- The only living things that are capable of flying are birds, bats and insects. While birds have been flying for millions of years, humans have only recently learned how to fly. They have used science to do this.

- Humans have invented kites, airships, gliders, air balloons, helicopters, fighter jets, commercial planes and supersonic flight.

- Supersonic flight is when an object flies faster than the speed of sound which is 1,235 kilometres per hour.

- Orville and Wilbur Wright were the first to fly in the air for 12 seconds, in 1903.

- The engine provides thrust which pushes the plane forward. The air goes over the wings which have a special shape. They help the airplane lift and overcome the pull of gravity.

Is it true?	yes	no
Humans have known how to fly for millions of years.	☐	☐
Humans have invented many different flying machines.	☐	☐
'Supersonic' means flying faster than the speed of sound.	☐	☐
The Wright brothers flew the first flying machine for 12 minutes.	☐	☐
The engine makes the airplane move forward.	☐	☐
The shape of the wings helps the airplane lift up.	☐	☐

Book 9: Comprehension quiz

Write the correct answer on the line.

1. The shard was sharp and cut Finn's _____.
a) arm   b) leg   c) hand   d) finger

2. People were imprisoned inside the _____
a) house   b) fortress   c) kitchen   d) mountain

3. Finn was bombarded by flying _____.
a) insects   b) stones   c) machines   d) clouds

4. The secret entrance into the fortress was an underwater _____.
a) tunnel   b) lane   c) street   d) wall

5. 'Artificial' means _____.
a) pretty   b) like art   c) not natural   d) fishy

6. 'Partially hidden' means only _____ hidden
a) fully   b) completely   c) not at all   d) partly

7. _____ made the engine corrode and stop working.
a) water   b) earth   c) pebbles   d) sea salt

8. The owner of the fortress told Finn he had great _____.
a) influence   b) happiness   c) potential   d) shoes

Book 9: Spelling assessment

-tial	**-cial**
initial	special
martial	social
potential	racial
spatial*	facial
torrential	official
substantial	financial
confidential	artificial
residential	beneficial

* Please note that spatial can also be spelled spacial.

This list can be used as a spelling assessment at the end of each unit of work. The teacher can add words from list 2 for able students. When dictating a word, say the word. Then say a sentence with the word in it (to put the word in the context of a sentence) and then repeat the word. E.g. "Rescue. I had to rescue the dog from the pond. Rescue." This ensures that the student has heard the word correctly. This sheet may be photocopied by the purchaser.
© Phonic Books Ltd 2016

Book 9 – Line-up game <cial>, <tial>

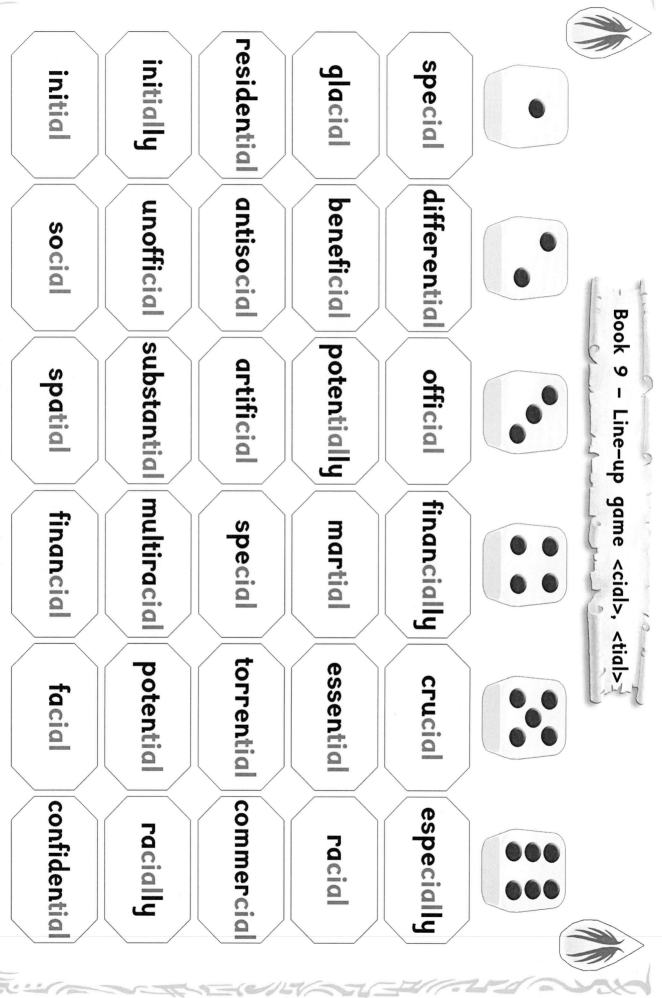

This game is for two players. Each player needs a batch of counters of one color. The players take turns to throw the die. They read a word in the column that corresponds to the number on the die and place their counter on that word. The first to have three of his/her counters in a row is the winner.

•	special	differential	official	financially	crucial	especially
••	glacial	beneficial	potentially	martial	essential	racial
•••	residential	antisocial	artificial	special	torrential	commercial
::	initially	unofficial	substantial	multiracial	potential	racially
⁙	initial	social	spatial	financial	facial	confidential

Book 10

Shattered Illusions

Suffix: <-sion>

Book 10: Blending and segmenting: <sion>

vision	v	i	sion			
division						
occasion						
version						
invasion						
decision						
confusion						
revision						
diversion						
inclusion						
precision						
collision						
television						

Blend the sounds and read the word. Segment the word into sounds by writing one sound in each square. This sheet may be photocopied by the purchaser. © Phonic Books Ltd 2016

Book 10: Reading and dictation <sion>

sion

vision	☐
revision	☐
decision	☐
illusion	☐
erosion	☐
version	☐
division	☐
occasion	☐
invasion	☐
incision	☐
derision	☐
precision	☐
inclusion	☐
exclusion	☐
confusion	☐

sion

Fold the page along the dotted line. Ask the student to read the words on the left-hand side of the page. She/he can put a check next to them as he/she reads them. Turn over the folded page and dictate the same words to the student. He/she then opens up the page and checks his/her spelling with words in the left-hand column. This page may be photocopied by the purchaser. © Phonic Books Ltd 2016

Book 10: Reading words with <sion>

vision 1	confusion 2	revision 3	decision 4
division 5	conclusion 6	precision 7	occasion 8
illusion 9	collision 10	explosion 11	intrusion 12

end 6	being accurate 7	rereading a subject before an exam 3	the act of sharing out or dividing something 5
when things are mixed up, unclear 2	a special event or time 8	something that seems real but is not real 9	an unwelcome visit 12
when something explodes 11	sight 1	a choice made after considering something	a crash 10

Photocopy this page onto card and cut out the words and the definitions. Match the definitions with the words, using the numbers and stick them back to back. Read and discuss the meanings of the words on the cards. This sheet may be photocopied by the purchaser.

Book 10: Reading words with <sion>

vision	confusion	revision	decision
division	conclusion	precision	occasion
illusion	collision	explosion	intrusion

end	being accurate	rereading a subject before an exam	the act of sharing out or dividing something
when things are mixed up, unclear	a special event or time	something that seems real but is not real	an unwelcome visit
when something explodes	sight	a choice made after considering something	a crash

Photocopy this page onto card and cut out the words and the definitions. Match the definitions with the words and stick them back to back. Read and discuss the meanings of the words on the cards. This sheet may be photocopied by the purchaser.

Book 10: Reading and spelling <sion>

sion

_____

_____

_____

_____

_____

_____

_____

_____

_____

_____

_____

_____

Reread Book 10 and find the words with the suffix <sion>. List these words in the column above.
This sheet may be photocopied by the purchaser. © Phonic Books Ltd 2016

Book 10: Chunking into syllables: <sion>

vision _____/_____

version _____/_____

decision _____/_____/_____

occasion _____/_____/_____

confusion _____/_____/_____

explosion _____/_____/_____

precision _____/_____/_____

illusion _____/_____/_____

collision _____/_____/_____

diversion _____/_____/_____

invasion _____/_____/_____

infusion _____/_____/_____

erosion _____/_____/_____

exclusion _____/_____/_____

persuasion _____/_____/_____

division _____/_____/_____

indecision _____/_____/_____/_____

Chunk the words into syllables and write the syllables on the lines. These words can also be used for dictation. This sheet may be photocopied by the purchaser. © Phonic Books Ltd 2016

Book 10: Questions for discussion

a) Finn said it was 'time for the conclusion of the quest'. What did he mean? (page 1)

b) What important information did Korus tell Finn? (page 2)

c) Why do you think Korus waited until the end of the quest to tell Finn that the Winged One was his brother? (page 2)

d) What was the Winged One's nest made of? (page 6)

e) What does Korus say to his brother? (pages 7, 8)

f) How did Korus get the skyshard from his brother? (page 9)

g) Titan's vision was restored. What does that mean? (page 11)

h) How did the Winged One use his army of crows? (page 12)

i) What did Finn think had happened to Korus? (page 14)

j) What do you think Finn and Korus will do next? (page 16)

This worksheet offers an opportunity to extend language and comprehension after reading Book 10. Discuss the questions above. Make sure the student understands and uses the new vocabulary in the book. This worksheet may be photocopied by the purchaser. © Phonic Books Ltd 2016

Book 10:   What's missing in the picture?

The sea shuddered with the force of Titan's mighty

blows. Scorching water shot from the geysers, hitting

the swarm of birds like a wall of molten heat. The dark

swarm retreated in fear. Finn stroked Korus's limp body.

Was this the end of his friend? His vision misted with

tears. But Korus was still breathing!

178

Book 10: Reading fluency

Titan rose to meet the challenge of the Winged One. His vision was restored and he saw Finn for the first time.

"I have the last skyshard, Titan!" yelled Finn as he rammed it into the gauntlets. Titan surged forward towards him. He was ready to take back his power from Finn.

With a high-pitched screech, the Winged One summoned his mighty army. The swarm of evil crows attacked Titan with military precision. This was what they had been trained for. Wave after wave of them pecked at his eyes, blacking out his vision. He stumbled heavily, shaken off balance.

| 1st reading _____ mins |
| 2nd reading _____ mins |
| 3rd reading _____ mins |

Finn leaped onto Titan and jammed the gauntlets into a socket in his chest. A glow of light appeared around Titan's stone hands. The gauntlets had returned to their rightful owner. He raised his arm and struck the Winged One with determined precision. The sea shuddered with the force from Titan's mighty blows. Scorching water shot from the geysers, hitting the swarm of birds like a wall of molten heat. The dark swarm retreated in fear.

Finn stroked Korus's limp body. Was this the end of his friend? His vision misted with tears, but Korus was still breathing!
"You're alive, Korus!" cried Finn, delighted.

| 1st reading _____ mins |
| 2nd reading _____ mins |
| 3rd reading _____ mins |

This worksheet develops reading fluency. Each text box has approximately 100 words, based on the story in the series. Fold the sheet on the dotted line. Ask the student to read the first passage three times. Each attempt is timed. In the following lesson, the teacher can ask the student to read the next passage or both passages to increase reading stamina. This sheet can be photocopied by the purchaser.
© Phonic Books Ltd 2016

Book 10: Punctuation

Capital letters, periods, exclamation marks and speech marks

Speech marks are used to show words that are spoken.

Remember to put any punctuation (like periods, commas and question marks) inside the speech marks.

to his horror, finn saw korus fall, lifeless, to the rotting timbers below

no screamed finn

the winged one howled in pain

i may have lost the skyshard, but i can still defeat titan with my army of crows he screeched

There are **9** capital letters, **4** speech marks, **2** exclamation marks and **4** periods missing.
Did you spot them all?

This is a punctuation and comprehension activity. Read the text carefully and find the missing periods, capital letters, exclamation marks and speech marks. This sheet may be photocopied by the purchaser. © Phonic Books Ltd 2016

Book 10: Writing activity 1

TITAN'S GAUNTLETS BOOK REVIEW

Who was your favorite character? Why?

_____

_____

_____

Which was your favorite book in the series? Why?

_____

_____

_____

What could be improved about the series?

_____

_____

_____

_____

Which age-group do you think will enjoy reading the series? Explain why.

_____

_____

_____

Would you recommend the series to your friends? Why?

_____

_____

_____

_____

Book 10: Writing activity 2

THE NEXT QUEST

At the end of Titan's Gauntlets, Finn and Korus watch Titan stride off into the horizon. Now that he has the skyshards safely back in the gauntlets, his powers have been restored. Titan can keep the world safe again.

If you were to write the next series, how would you start it? Would Finn and Korus be in it? Would Titan be in it? Would you introduce new characters? Where would it take place? What would happen in your story?

Write the first chapter of your story.

_____

_____

_____

_____

_____

_____

_____

_____

_____

_____

_____

_____

_____

_____

_____

Book 10: New vocabulary – cloze activity

1. **harness** – to make effective use of something
2. **persuasion** – persuading someone
3. **illusion** – having a wrong impression of reality
4. **collision** – crash
5. **intrusion** – coming in without invitation
6. **conclusion** – end
7. **debris** – scattered pieces of rubbish or remains

Finn realized he had reached the _____ of the quest. He gazed about him. The sea was littered with _____.

"Sorry for the _____," said Korus. Korus explained that the Winged One was actually his brother. He had stolen the skyshards from Titan. The Winged One had kept one skyshard but scattered the rest across the ocean. He planned to _____ their power. Now Korus came face to face with his brother.

"So, Chosen One!" spat the Winged One.

"Brother, give up the _____ of power!" Korus tried to reason with his brother, but it was no use. He made one last attempt at _____. When the army of crows attacked Finn, Korus went for the Winged One. There was a mighty _____ as the two birds fought.

Book 10: Comprehension – True or false?

Crows

Crows are millions of years old. They live everywhere on Earth except Antarctica. There are over 40 different types of crows. They belong to a bird family called Corvids, which includes ravens and magpies.

Crows are classified as songbirds, but they don't sound like songbirds. They have different calls that communicate to other crows about territory, food and danger. Did you know that crows in captivity can learn to talk? In the wild, they can live up to 10 years. In captivity, they can live to 30 years. They are omnivores, which means that they eat everything: vegetables, insects, seeds and meat. They also eat carrion which is meat from dead animals.

Farmers don't like crows because they think that crows eat their seeds and crops. That is why they make scarecrows to scare them away. But actually, crows don't damage their crops that much. In fact, they eat the insects that damage their crops. Crows are the most intelligent birds in the world. They are not fooled by the scarecrows and are clever enough to know that they are not real human beings. Crows hide food in safe places. If another crow sees them, they pretend to hide food in one place, but then go and hide it somewhere else. They are so smart that they can make tools like bending a wire to get some food. They have been seen to place a nut in the road so that a car will crack it open for them. They can even recognize human faces.

Is it true?

	yes	no
Crows belong to the same family of birds as ravens and magpies.	☐	☐
Crows live longer in the wild.	☐	☐
'Omnivore' means eats everything.	☐	☐
Crows are scared of scarecrows.	☐	☐
Crows can make tools to get their food.	☐	☐
Crows can tell people apart.	☐	☐

Book 10: Comprehension quiz

Write the correct answer on the line.

1. The 'conclusion' of the quest means the _____ of the quest.
a) beginning   b) start   c) middle   d) end

2. 'Debris' means scattered _____.
a) food   b) people   c) rubbish   d) things

3. The Winged One was Korus's _____.
a) father   b) brother   c) uncle   d) twin

4. The black mist was a swarm of _____.
a) bees   b) wasps   c) bats   d) crows

5. 'Collision' means a _____.
a) crash   b) splash   c) gurgle   d) dive

6. Titan got his power back from the shards in the _____.
a) sword   b) axe   c) gauntlets   d) shield

7. 'Precision' means _____.
a) happiness   b) laziness   c) accuracy   d) hopefulness

8. The story about Titan's Gauntlets is a _____.
a) fantasy   b) report   c) diary   d) advertisement

Book 10: Spelling assessment

–sion

vision

revision

division

confusion

explosion

exclusion

inclusion

invasion

occasion

This list can be used as a spelling assessment at the end of each unit of work. The teacher can add words from list 2 for able students. When dictating a word, say the word. Then say a sentence with the word in it (to put the word in the context of a sentence) and then repeat the word. E.g. "Rescue. I had to rescue the dog from the pond. Rescue." This ensures that the student has heard the word correctly. This sheet may be photocopied by the purchaser.

Book 10 – Line-up game <sion>

1	2	3	4	5	6
vision	division	decision	television	occasion	confusion
revision	precision	erosion	illusion	inclusion	collision
persuasion	intrusion	indecision	exclusion	version	invasion
explosion	fusion	collision	diversion	transfusion	indecision
derision	occasion	invasion	erosion	precision	revision

This game is for two players. Each player needs a batch of counters of one color. The players take turns to throw the die. They read a word in the column that corresponds to the number on the die and place their counter on that word. The first to have three of his/her counters in a row is the winner.

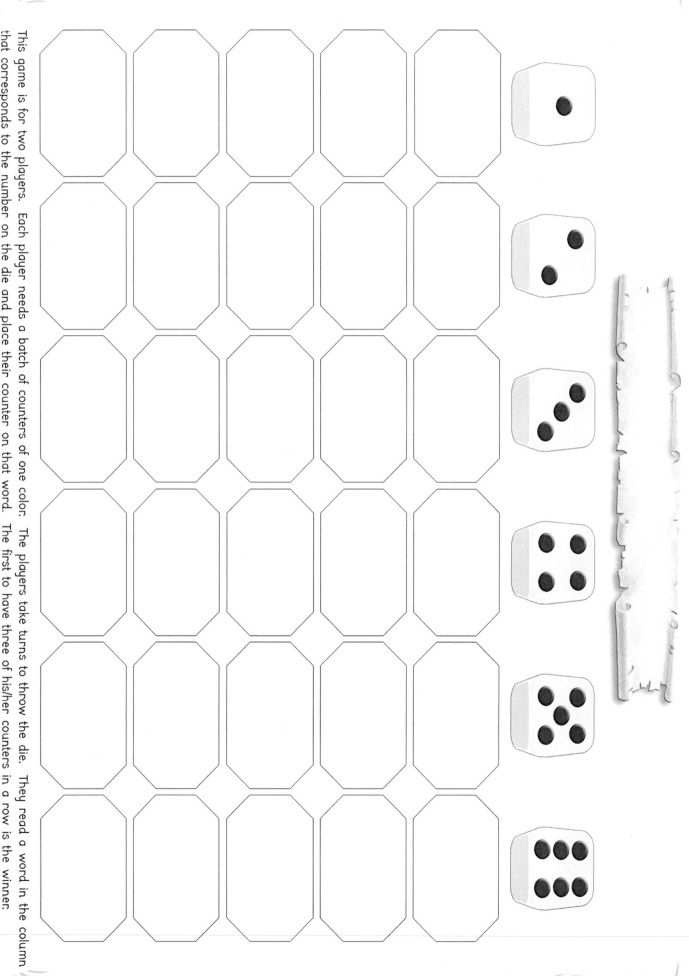

This game is for two players. Each player needs a batch of counters of one color. The players take turns to throw the die. They read a word in the column that corresponds to the number on the die and place their counter on that word. The first to have three of his/her counters in a row is the winner.